It Came from Beneath the Waves

It Came from Beneath the Waves

Weird Tales from the Ocean Depths

Edited by Matthew Pegg

First published in the UK in 2018 by Mantle Lane Press

ISBN 978-1-9998416-3-8

Mantle Lane Press
Mantle Arts
Springboard Centre
Mantle Lane
Coalville
LE67 3DW
www.mantlelanepress.co.uk
www.red-lighthouse.org.uk

Cover image by Zoe Murphy
www.zoemurphy.com

Contents

Introduction 7

The Selkie 9
Joanne Harris

Eqalussuaq 13
Tim Major

Bight, Tomcat and the Moon 35
Carmen Marcus

The King Tide 45
Alex Reece Abbott

Fillet 54
Liz Wride

Harris 64
Pauline Jérémie

When It Sleets 68
Sarah Leavesley

Beachsidepotter 73
Susan E Barsby

Seal Boy 80
Sarah Evans

The Sea Inside 94
Linda Maclennan

The Men of the Nets 112
Lydia McGill

The Writers 120
Acknowledgements 124

Introduction

The ocean has always beguiled and terrified us. Essential to life on earth and as hostile an enviornment as deep space, it provides us with sustcnance and life, and can also obliterate us. No wonder then that stories of the sea and the things that may lurk beneath it are as old as the human race itself. From sea serpents that adorned early maps through to folk tales of seal people and mermaids, we have always wondered what lurks beneath the surface of the ocean, and spun tales about it.

This collection of stories contains some strange creatures. But more than stories of outside threats, it looks at our relationships with each other, reflected in the mirror of the ocean. Here you'll find horror stories, but also post apolcalyptic science fiction, historical tales and contemporary fiction from a wide range of exciting authors.

So come and find out what lurks beneath the waves.

'Here Be Monsters.'

Some of them are us.

The Selkie
Joanne Harris

There once was a girl of the travelling folk, of the clan they call the selkie. Her people were the folk of the sea; the dolphin; the sea-lion; the seal and the whale. The selkie were a warrior clan, fighting the Folk who lived on the land; hunted, and hunting, and happy, and free. But the travelling girl was not happy. She dreamed of the land, with its heathery hills, and its open fields of swaying grass. And when her people hunted for the shoals of herring out to sea, the selkie girl would watch the Folk, and follow them from afar, and dream.

Her people said: 'Beware the Folk. They hunt and kill our children. They flay us, and they wear our skins, and they cannot be trusted.'

But the girl would not listen, and at night, would swim to the islands of the Folk, and leave her sealskin on the shore, and walk alone on the cool sand. Sometimes she looked into their homes, and watched them with their children, and dreamed of having a hearth, and a family, far away from the cold north sea.

Then, one night, a young man of the Folk was walking alone on the seashore. He was the son of a gunnerman on a whaling-ship out to sea, and he dreamed of the open waves, and the scent of blood on the spray. And the young man saw the selkie girl, standing naked by the shore, and saw that she was beautiful. Night after night he watched her there, but she was too wild to come to him. And so he went to his mother, and told her of the selkie girl, and of his great desire for her.

The mother told him: 'Bring me the sealskin that she leaves every night by the water's edge. Without it, she will not remember the sea.'

And so the boy stole the sealskin, and gave it to his mother, who hid it in the cedar chest in which she kept her wedding-dress. Then he went back to the seashore, and found the selkie girl naked and afraid on the beach, with no memory of how she had come to be there.

The selkie girl, knowing nothing except that the young man was kind, followed him to his mother's house. As time passed, she grew to love the young man. And yet, there was something about the mother's house that troubled her. Maybe it was the great harpoon mounted on the wall, or the carved ivories, or the sealskins. But she could not remember why these things disturbed her.

Time passed. The gunnerman returned from his time of the whaling-ship, and took his son to sea with him, promising to be back by spring. And the mother and the selkie girl went every day to the market to sell the skins and ivories that the gunnerman had brought. The girl hated the market, with its stench of death, and yet could not remember why she felt such horror at the sealskins. By midwinter she found herself with child, and fretted and wept for her young man's return. But the mother was delighted, and said: 'Be patient, child, and you shall be wed. When my son comes home from the sea, you shall wear my wedding-dress, kept safe in the cedar chest.'

But the girl, now heavy with child, feared that the dress would not fit her. So one night, in secret, she opened the chest and took it out. The sealskin was lying under the dress, half-hidden beneath the embroidered silk. As soon as her fingers touched the skin, the mother's spell was broken and her memory of the selkie returned. Horrified at how she had been used, she ran to the beach and called her folk in the language of her clan.

Their chieftain came at her call, and the girl begged him, weeping, to take her back. 'Wait until the baby is born,' said the selkie chieftain. 'Then you may return to our folk, as long as you have your sealskin.'

The girl waited eagerly for the time when she could escape and return to the sea. Every night she looked into the chest, to make sure the sealskin was still there.

And then at last, her babe was born: a brown-eyed son with eyes like a seal's.

But when the girl ran to the cedar chest to take out her seal-skin and escape, the sealskin was no longer there. The mother, scenting mischief, had cut it up and fashioned it into a pair of mittens and a hunting-cap for her husband.

The girl cried out in horror, but the mother simply laughed. 'Now you can never escape,' she said. 'You'll be a slave forever.'

The girl ran down to the beach again, and called for the clan of the selkie. She handed them the infant, saying: 'Take him far away from here. Keep him safe. Teach him to love the ocean.' And then she went back to the gunnerman's house, and stood in the door with her hair in her eyes.

The gunnerman's wife laughed at her. 'Did you not understand?' she said. 'Without your sealskin, you cannot change.'

'You have made me a slave,' said the girl. 'But though I cannot escape, I can change.' And then she killed the gunnerman's wife, and took her skin, and put it on, and took her form, and sat in her chair and waited. She waited for the gunnerman and his son to return from the sea. And then she killed them both, and collected their skins, and gave them to the selkie. Unrecognized, the selkie walked among the Folk in the likeness of the gunnerman and his son, collecting more skins as they went. And there they still walk unseen to this day; in markets and on whaling-ships, collecting the hides of the enemy. The Folk call them the Craiceann – skin-changers - or sometimes, the Kraken, and many tales are told of them.

Most of these tales are untrue. But one thing is known: the selkie's child never returned to the land of his birth. He remained far away, in the warm south seas, living free and happy among the pilot whales, the sea turtles and dolphins.

Eqalussuaq
Tim Major

As Lea had predicted, Peter threw a tantrum the instant he threw open the front door to find her standing on the step. She bent and scooped him into her arms, he shuddered against her. She had imagined that he would be taller, visibly older, in the twelve weeks that had passed. If anything, he seemed to have become lighter.

'Don't fret, now,' she said. 'Mum's back.'

Peter buried his face into her shoulder, depositing mucus onto her cardigan. More like a newborn than a six-year-old. His blonde hair had begun to sneak over the tips of his ears.

With her usual tact, Lea's friend Karen had already stepped soundlessly into the lounge, leaving mother and son to their reunion. Lea closed the front door with her hip and entered Karen's house. Peter regained his calm but still said nothing. He wriggled free of Lea's embrace to sit close beside Karen on the sofa. Anyone might have assumed she was his mother, not Lea.

'So. Tell me,' Lea said.

Karen wrinkled her nose. 'I won't lie. It was tougher this time. But we had our fair share of fun. Didn't we?' She rubbed Peter's head but he shrugged her away in order to glare at Lea.

'And at school?'

'Worse. More biting. Poor Daphne's parents said they'll call.'

Lea winced. Stains marked Peter's cheeks, though he wasn't

crying. Old tears.

'Peter, listen,' she said, 'What did we agree, before I left? About how you treat other children?'

Peter only shook his head. Based on past experience, it would take days for him to thaw. Until then, he would be impenetrable. An iceberg.

'That's not all,' Karen said. 'I couldn't think how to tell you by email. Last week, Thursday, he ran away. I was frantic.' Her hands began to tremble. Lea glanced down and saw that her own hands shook a little, too. 'The whole island helped me search for him. We found him in one of the refuge huts out on the causeway. He'd been trapped there for hours, Lea.'

A shudder ran through Lea's body. She felt chill sting her skin, then seem to penetrate to her bones in an instant. 'Thursday? The fourteenth?' she said, her jaw tight to stop her teeth chattering. 'You're sure?'

Karen shrugged. 'Pretty sure.'

Lea examined her friend's expression. There was concern there, but it was directed at Peter, rather than Lea herself. The news mustn't have reached Britain yet. Or maybe the media didn't judge the story as dramatic as it had seemed first-hand.

She glanced at Peter. What was the appropriate parental response to the news about his attempted escape from Lindisfarne? A mother ought to know, instinctively.

On the fourteenth of September, when she had slipped beneath the water, perhaps for the last time ever, she reflected now, the cold had seemed more absolute than it ought. She had felt a sudden shock of fear then, during that solo dive, easily comparable to the fear she experienced during the incident later that day. Perhaps it had been a response to danger back at home. Perhaps she had a maternal instinct, after all.

'You understand, don't you?' Karen said. She was choosing

her words carefully, too. Forcing herself not to scold Lea in front of her son. 'He wasn't trying to get away, so much as he was trying to get closer to what he wanted. He was trying to follow you.'

Lea made her excuses to Karen, with vague arrangements to meet later in the week. As she stepped over the threshold, Karen gripped her arm.

'I know it was an important trip for you,' she said. 'I understand why you went. And it's not that I mind having him here. You're closer to me than my sister, and Peter's like a son. But three whole months, Lea, and not a single phone call from you… I can't do that again, okay? Not for a while.'

Lea nodded and shuffled into the street with her shivering child.

It was only when Peter had finally fallen asleep that Lea had the chance to check the contents of her duffel bag. She pushed aside the thick parka and dirty laundry to retrieve the hard black case beneath. Inside, six portable hard drives made a neat row. Throughout the journey she had suffered from paranoia; all those weeks of work contained within something so easily lost. On the bumpy flight from Ilulissat she had woken shouting from a doze, certain that some atmospheric phenomenon had wiped the drives.

She booted her computer, slipped out the first drive, and ran a backup. She exhaled fully for the first time in days. Safe and sound.

When all of the backups had finished, she glanced towards the staircase. No sounds from Peter. Guiltily, she slipped on her headphones. If he yelled now, she wouldn't hear it.

She selected a file at random and clicked play. A waveform appeared onscreen, reassuring in its dark fluidity. Her eyes narrowed as she concentrated on the skittering sound. Onscreen, a dark peak broke up and away, matching a corresponding sound in the headphones. She smiled. The call of a black-legged kittiwake. Her thighs had ached terribly after she had crouched for hours with her rifle mic pointed at the nest.

She chose another track. Instantly, her headphones filled with a burping, chuckling noise. She checked the filename against the handwritten description in her notebook. Earless harp seals, slithering on the ice as they huddled together.

She settled into the swivel chair, sipping wine as she browsed through the tracks. Her hands shook only a little now, the lingering fear subsiding. The tracks were all pristine. A month of good work.

The most recently-used drive was easily identifiable, as its surface was scuffed and scratched. When she had awoken in the hut on the fifteenth, she had insisted that it be found and brought to her immediately. When she had finally made herself understood to the Inuit guides who watched over her, and they had relayed the message to her colleagues, and the hard drive had been located, she had cursed at Nils for allowing it to be handled so roughly. The look on her producer's face as he handed it over was easy to read. *After what's happened,* his expression said, *you're worried about the work?*

She had earned her reputation as a killjoy early on in the expedition. Of the seven-man team, she was the only one who refused to play along with the in-jokes about the island where they had been based for the first fortnight, insisting on using its Greenlandic title, Qeqertarsuaq, rather than the anglicised Disko Island. She had asked for the Earth, Wind and Fire to be turned down during the jeep ride from the airport. She had complained to Nils when someone had scrawled *disko sucks* in Tipp-Ex on one arm of her wetsuit. And when, on the first day of work proper, her first hard drive of sound recordings had been replaced with another containing only one track, a repeated twenty-second loop of the Bee Gees singing 'Staying Alive', she had thrown a tantrum that would have awed her six-year-old son.

She didn't care then and she didn't care now. She had the files.

She hooked up the most recent hard drive and selected the first track, labelled *14Sep16_001*. Her two glasses of wine had left her a little drunk. She raised her hands like a conductor as the track played.

It began with a gulp. The sound of her own body slipping into the water, probably. She shivered now. Hadn't the thought passed through her mind, at that moment, of Peter's fate if she were to freeze there in Baffin Bay? Even at the time she had recognised the thought as uncharacteristic. If she was being honest, she hadn't thought about Peter a great deal, up to that point in the expedition. But being alone in icy water, far from assistance, might make anyone behave oddly. From underwater she had looked at the towering iceberg above, its edges knife-sharp from its recent calving from the Jakobshavn glacier. Refraction had made it bend towards her. She had felt impossibly fragile.

Bubbling sounds followed. Her last exhalation before she had settled herself into position. As the bubbles ceased, the background sounds became more easily audible. Lea leant forward to turn up the amp.

The creaking sound reminded her of her grandmother's rocking chair against wooden floorboards. Except there were layers beneath. A sighing, a throb of life. The quiet belch of bubbles released from somewhere in the depths, pushing along the underside of the iceberg before finding freedom at the water's surface. The rumble and snap of the iceberg itself as its regions thawed or refroze. An embrace of womb-like warmth that eclipsed the physical memory of the water's icy chill.

It was good. A beautiful, living sound in its own right, as well as fulfilling producer Nils' brief of demonstrating the rate of thaw for the TV documentary. Lea sipped wine and conducted the orchestra of creaks and burbles. It was good.

Even back then, floating twenty feet down, she had had the distinct thought, *This is the best yet.* Then, as she had stifled her shivers in order to hold the microphone tight and to track the fast-moving iceberg, *This might be the best work I ever do.*

At the time.

By lunchtime, during the team meeting at the tiny base situated north of Ilulissat, a new opportunity had presented itself. An achievement that might easily surpass the glacier groans.

The second camerawoman, Reeta, was first to notice the change in the Inuit guide, Sighna. She interrupted Nils' summary of footage gathered that morning to rush over to Sighna and steady him, preventing him from toppling into the open brazier in the centre of the hut. Lea and the others watched in silence as Reeta tried to grasp Sighna's hands. He wrenched them away and pressed them to either side of his head. He shook as though he were trying to squeeze his skull. He hissed a word, again and again and again. 'Eqalussuaq.'

Nils tried to speak to Reeta, but she waved him away. He returned to stand next to Lea, his arms folded. He had never been good at inaction. Some other members of the team moved away from Sighna and Reeta, too, similarly embarrassed.

'Eqalussuaq,' Nils whispered.

'What does it mean?' Lea asked.

'It's a name,' Nils said. 'Or two names, depending how you think about it.'

They watched as Reeta helped Sighna to sit and gathered rucksacks to make a cushioned throne.

Nils continued, 'I read the name first in a book of Greenlandic legends. Kind of a cute one. Some old woman washed her hair in urine – I know, go figure – then dried it with a cloth, which then sailed away on the wind, into the ocean. It became Ekalugsuak, and its descendants, Eqalussuaq.'

The first-unit director, Terence, was listening. He stuck out his tongue. 'So what's the significance of this progeny of a piss-cloth, then?'

'It'll be of interest to you, Terry, professionally speaking,' Nis replied. 'Eqalussuaq is an animal. The Greenland shark.'

Lea saw Terence's eyes widen. He turned to Reeta, still kneeling beside the Inuit guide, whose lips were moving even though his voice had quietened. 'Hey. Hey. Ask him why he's saying that word.'

Sighna looked up blearily as Reeta asked the question in Greenlandic. He lifted his hands from his ears, only for a moment. He spoke in a voice too low for Lea to hear.

Reeta turned. 'He says it's close. No, that's not quite the word. I don't know. Exalted? High up.'

'Shitting hell,' Terence said. 'Meaning the Greenland shark is close? Does he know that for a fact?'

The guide was still speaking to Reeta, his lips trembling as he spoke. Reeta frowned and nodded, her palm raised to the man, perhaps as a signal for him to remain calm.

'What's the deal?' Lea whispered to Nils. 'What's so exciting?'

Nils pressed his hand on his face, drawing it downwards until his jowls bounced. 'It's the biggest bastard out there. Twenty-plus feet and with the oldest living to two hundred years. It's notorious, but partly that's just because of the toxicity of the flesh: remember in the port bar last night, I told you the natives use the phrase 'shark-sick' to mean drunk?'

Reeta stood up. She glanced at Sighna, who had slumped back into the pile of rucksacks. 'It's all a bit of a jumble. My translation skills…' She blinked, perhaps registering the expressions of her team members. 'Sighna says the shark coming close always affects him in this way. Says his head hurts, it's hard to concentrate. I'm not sure I'm getting this right, but he's complaining about something loud. Shouting. Maybe screaming.'

Terence held her by the shoulders. 'And the shark? He thinks it's nearby?'

'He's positive. Although I don't know why you'd treat that as…'

'Where?' Terence was already packing gear into a bag. He whistled to get the attention of the assistant director and another of the cameramen, who were deep in conversation at the far side of the hut.

'All the way back where Lea was this morning,' Reeta said. 'Right at the foot of the Jakobshavn glacier.'

Terence and Nils exchanged glances. After a few moments, Nils shrugged his approval. 'I'll buzz the boat crew. We'll meet them as close as we can get.'

Lea started gathering her kit, too. 'I'll show you the way down to the water.' She turned to Nils. 'So this shark's a catch, right? A rarity?'

Nils' face had turned pale. 'Like you wouldn't believe. They almost never show their ugly faces. If one's come close to the surface…'

She was first in the jeep, turning over the engine and gesticulating orders for the other team members to hurry.

Lea pulled off her headphones and listened for Peter. Still no sound. She scrolled down the filenames on the hard drive. The filesize of the final track was enormous. Whoever had been operating it remotely from the boat must have let the recording run on, afterwards, while she was being hauled out of the sea. Her index finger paused over the mouse button. She turned in her swivel chair and lifted the phone.

The call went to voice mail. She hung up and tried again. This time, after several rings, Nils answered.

'It's Lea. I need to see it.'

'Lea? It's… what time is it?'

'I don't know. Late, I guess. Can you send me the footage?'

'Jesus. Are you alright?'

'I'm just not tired, that's all. Got back this afternoon.'

'That's not what I meant and you know it. How are you? I thought they were going to keep you in longer.'

'It was only concussion, and I couldn't bear it any longer. It was so cold. Hospitals are never cold.' Lea shuddered at the thought of her bare feet against the cold, tiled floor of the ward at Queen Ingrid's Hospital.

A pause. 'Have you spoken to anyone?'

'I'm not a talker. You?'

'Yeah. I mean, of course. My wife, kids, my two best friends. I spoke to Carl on the phone, too, as soon as I got home. Two days too late to be anywhere near the first to offer commiserations, of course, but—' Abruptly, the phone line hummed with static. It took a few seconds for Lea to realise that Nils was sobbing. 'Fuck. Lea. Carl was— I don't know. He refused to blame me. Said I'll be welcome at her funeral. But… Reeta was part of my team. She was my responsibility. If it wasn't my fault, then I don't know who. And then there was almost you, too.'

'Almost.' Lea tested the word 'blame' in her mind, holding it up against herself and her own actions. 'But I'm okay. I am.'

'I'm glad,' Nils said, sniffing. 'I'm so glad. If you ever need anything, Lea…'

'I just need you to send me the footage.'

The jeep skidded to a halt at the coast. Lea leapt out, jogging to the shore, scanning for corpses. Terence ran at her side, barely able to contain his glee at the prospect of discovering a bear or seal, evidence of one of Eqalussuaq's rare forays above the surface. During the jeep journey, Nils had pulled up Google image results of seals found with rips that corkscrewed around their bodies. As she had glanced at the photos, Lea's only thought had been to wonder what the attack must have sounded like.

They found nothing but the waiting boat. Its three crew members took Nils aside to speak to him, before allowing any of the production team on board. Even then, they remained far quieter than usual.

For three hours, the boat bobbed in the waters at the foot of the Jakobshavn glacier. After the first hour, Lea's eyes grew tired of staring at the roiling waters and her stomach ached from leaning over the rail. She gazed up at the glacier and imagined that she could make out its creep, pushing across the sea towards the boat.

When Reeta volunteered to go below the surface, Lea stood at her side and insisted that she should go too. She held the microphone before her like a staff, as if to demonstrate her strength. Nils protested, of course, but Lea made her case again and again. If Eqalussuaq wasn't down there, then she could simply gather more iceberg and background recordings. And if it was, then wouldn't it be a crime to have video footage but no sound?

Lea refreshed her inbox until the email appeared. She followed the link to the fileshare site. While she waited for it to download, she darted upstairs to fetch a blanket, then drank another glass of wine huddled beneath it. It was getting colder all the time.

She opened the final sound file, *14Sep16_044*, then clicked the pause button before it started.

The video finished downloading. She set it running. The video was far from broadcast quality, as it was the backup from the remote feed the rest of the team had viewed on the boat, rather than the master files. After a dizzying flurry of pixel artefacts and indigo bubbles, the image cleared a little. She saw herself, barely recognisable in her wetsuit, identifiable only by the Tippex marks on her shoulder: *disko sucks*.

Onscreen, she held up three fingers. Here, now, Lea copied the pose, then two fingers, then one. Then she clicked the play button on the sound file.

Suddenly, the bubbles produced by her scuba equipment were accompanied by gulping sounds through the headphones. Lea leant close to the screen, trying to judge whether sound and image matched. The underwater Lea tapped on the microphone, twice, producing dull thuds. Perfect sync.

It was as she remembered. Reeta's camera swung smoothly around, performing a three-sixty turn to end up facing Lea again. Lea gesticulated and Reeta spun quicker, losing her balance. Lea shook her head. She hadn't meant to suggest that she had seen anything that should be filmed, she had only meant to tell Reeta to point the camera somewhere other than towards her.

The gurgling sound increased in volume, the only clue that Lea had allowed herself to descend further. Reeta's camera dropped too and the indigo screen darkened. When the bubbles lessened once again, Lea could hear the low grumbles and creaks of the icebergs above.

It was difficult to remember how long they had floated there, searching the darkness for signs of the shark. Even now, watching onscreen, Lea lost track. Her eyelids drooped. If it hadn't been so cold, she might have slept.

A flurry of bubbles alerted her. The video artefacted again as Reeta bounced the camera around. When it stabilised, Lea could see herself once more, in the bottom left-hand corner of the screen, barely visible against the blackness of the lower depths. This tiny Lea was looking up and away from Reeta's camera.

And then there it was.

Eqalussuaq.

Lea felt a swell of disappointment. Even with its entire length visible, the shark seemed squat and small, making a horizontal stripe across the centre-left of the screen. Its tail was only a few pixels in height. She tried to judge the distance between her and it. Ten feet? Five? Both of them seemed to fidget, an effect of the camera shaking.

The shark seemed to hover before Lea, maintaining a consistent distance. The effect was as though it were tethered to her like a balloon. Onscreen, Lea stretched out her arm, pushing the microphone towards the thing. New sounds came from the headphones. Whooshes and hisses. Its fins as it adjusted its position.

Then, both Lea and the shark seemed to grow. Reeta was moving closer. Brave girl. For the first time, Lea felt a stab of guilt about what happened next.

It would be any second now.

The shark edged backwards – she hadn't realised that at the time – before it leapt towards Lea. Her arm lifted to protect her face, producing loud gulps as the weight of the water pushed back against the microphone. Then, onscreen, Lea's head raised to look directly at the shark as it came.

She remembered the sequence of events clearly, up to a point. Her memories filled in what the grainy footage had failed to capture.

She remembered seeing the thin threads that trailed from each of its eyes. Nils had described them during the jeep journey: parasites that itched and blinded the shark.

She remembered the moment in which the shark seemed to travel above her, rather than towards her, before its jaw dropped open.

She remembered the distinct difference between its two sets of teeth: broad and square below, thin and pointed above. An ugly phrase had repeated in her mind: seal ripping.

She remembered opening her mouth just as the shark did, releasing her grip on her scuba mouthpiece, and letting loose a storm of bubbles that almost, but not quite, obscured Eqalussuaq, and she remembered shouting at it. The recording failed to capture the words, but she spoke them aloud, again, now.

'Not me! Take her!'

Abruptly, a squall of sound shrieked through the headphones. Lea spasmed and one arm knocked the glass from the worktop, spraying red wine onto the screen. She ripped the headphones from her ears.

Onscreen, the open jaws of the shark shuddered, as if the shriek came from within.

What was *that?* Instinctively, she glanced at the waveform. Its shape was smoothly bulbous, without peaks.

She bent the headphone cup to listen with one ear. The shriek began again, even louder than before. Even with the amp dialled down, she could hardly bear to hear it. Now she could make out a guttural growl beneath the shrill static.

She flung the headphones down again.

Onscreen, silent, the shark turned. Now it faced the camera full on.

Perhaps Reeta wasn't so brave, after all. At the moment that it was clear that Eqalussuaq was accelerating towards her, she let go of the camera. The blue light of the screen flashed bright and dark, bright and dark, as the camera spun and dropped down, down, down.

Upstairs, Peter began to howl.

She slept badly, imagining herself in the depths along with the abandoned camera. Something was down there with her, sinuous and sleek. It was a bad joke, she thought when she woke. Eqalussuaq, of the family Somniosidae. *Sleeper shark.*

The bulky headphones comforted her. As she strode towards the island's coast, she listened to the live recording stream from the binaural microphones fixed to the exterior of the earphone cups. Her footsteps redoubled in her ears, lagging fractionally behind the real world, as if following her.

Lindisfarne could be defined by its sounds: the wind tumbling from the sea and up the rock outcrops, the cries of the gulls and the whip of their wings, the dense, tactile calm within the oasis of the priory ruins. Captured and suitably arranged, it all belonged to Lea.

Her pace quickened as she headed through the sand dunes to the pebble beach, putting distance between herself and home. The Arctic recordings weren't scheduled to be delivered to Nils for another week, after Reeta's funeral, and indexing the sound files would involve only a handful of hours of work. That morning, when she had returned from delivering Peter to school, she had lingered in front of the computer, unable to bring herself to boot it up. Eqalussuaq's shriek had still echoed in her ears.

She had decided to distract herself by concentrating on other projects. Her record label had shown only muted interest in her proposal of manipulated ambient recordings from Lindisfarne, but they hadn't heard even the raw audio yet. Following post-production work in the studio, the tracks could be wonderful.

She was still crouching beside an abandoned boat, leaning in with the binaural mics to capture its dull scrape against the pebbles, when she noted the time. All those weeks away from home had left her insensitive to the timing of the tides. She would have to rush to make it across the causeway and back before the sea made it impassable.

As she turned from the shore a faint sound registered in her headphones. She turned to the boat again. Had its hull made that screech? She turned her head from side to side to locate the direction. It was coming from somewhere out at sea. Shrill. As the high-pitched noise grew in volume, she heard a deep grumble beneath, and she thought of icebergs. She stared out at the water, half-expecting to see a disturbance, something cutting through the waves as it approached.

Nothing. At least, nothing visible.

But the volume increased, all the same. The screech and roar became more insistent. Louder.

Angrier.

After another ten seconds she could no longer bear the shrieking. She pulled off the headphones and sprinted back towards the dunes.

Lea sat opposite Peter at the melamine table. He hadn't touched his burger. There were dark shadows beneath his eyes. After the awkwardness of the apology to Daphne and her parents at the school gates, Lea had brought him to a McDonald's in Berwick, but her desperation to maintain the pretence that it was a treat was wearing thin. Peter was a smart six-year-old. He understood that her delay on the island, and the high tide that now covered the Lindisfarne causeway, meant an enforced wait of four hours before they could return home.

'What if you'd got lost when you were away?' Peter said.

Lea flinched. Once again, she imagined herself freezing in Baffin Bay. If she'd found herself trapped down there, would she have prayed for Peter or would her final thoughts have been of her precious recordings?

'I had maps and people to show me around,' she said. She noted the petulance in her own voice.

'But you were far, far away.'

'Eat your food.'

Peter pushed away the greasy container. 'Daphne said you weren't coming back.'

'And that's why you bit her?'

'I bit her because she's a bitch.'

Lea sprung from her seat. 'Don't you dare use that kind of language!' She hovered beside him. What was she going to do, hit him?

Peter slumped further into his chair.

Lea sighed. It was fruitless to wonder where he'd learnt the word. She had no idea how he'd been living for the last three months. She would never have thought him capable of running away from home.

'Look,' she said, 'I was far away, you're right. But I found my way back to you, didn't I?'

Peter's sullen expression changed to one of quiet hope. 'Like I've got a homing beacon? So you can always find me?'

'Exactly. I zoomed across the seas, from Greenland all the way back to here. And I won't leave you again.' Instantly, she regretted the last part.

That night, after Peter had bathed, he insisted that Lea bring the portable radio into his bedroom. Karen, it transpired, had taken to leaving a radio on low volume, following a phase of interrupted sleep. The mutter of Radio 4 voices was unintelligible but soothing nonetheless, despite the static that wouldn't quite abate, no matter where Lea tuned the dial.

Shadows in the depths. Smooth skin and sharp points.

Lea woke in a panic.

That shriek again. It pulsated, echoing around the walls and in her head.

She burst into the corridor and down the stairs. Behind her, Peter's shouts mingled with the scream that seemed to come from everywhere at once.

The shrill sound was even louder as she neared her studio at the back of the house. She staggered with the pressure of it as she entered the room. The huge bookshelf speakers emitted waves of piercing white noise.

Lea lunged up at them. Once they were turned off, her body slumped in delayed shock.

She ignored Peter's wails. In the kitchen she turned on the radio, then flicked it off as the squealing sound began again. The TV in the lounge gave the same result, though the picture was unaffected.

It was everywhere.

With shaking hands, she booted up the computer. She opened one of the iceberg sound recordings at random.

She saw what had happened immediately. Instead of a smooth waveform, the sound editor showed a single block of black, with only occasional slices missing, like shards calved from an iceberg. Tentatively, she lifted the headphones and pressed play. The scream was unbearable, even with the headphones held at arm's length. The plastic buzzed and shook with the force of the sound.

She opened more and more sound files. They all appeared identical—masses of noise, black blots on the screen.

All of the recordings were gone. All of the sounds, eclipsed by a single shout. A shriek. A scream.

'No,' she whimpered. 'Please. Anything but this.'

She staggered backwards. The loss of the recordings felt like grief.

She remembered how the sound had approached as she had stood on the shore of the island. A phrase from the day before echoed in her mind.

…across the seas, from Greenland all the way back to here…

She thought of Sighna, the Inuit guide, his hands clamped over his ears.

She thought of Eqalussuaq, its jaws wide. Its silent scream, back then. Its shriek, on the recordings.

Whatever she had picked up on her microphone, it hadn't been a sound, not in the usual sense. It was something else. Something that she had trapped, or that had – what was the word? Hidden? No… burrowed. Torn and ripped and burrowed, hiding itself within her recordings.

And she had brought it home.

The bookshelf speakers began to rock. Lea shuddered. She could still hear the sound, though only faintly. She pulled the plug from the wall. The sound only grew in intensity.

Anger.

She felt an icy chill all over her body. The sound grew and grew and grew, dizzying, nauseating. It no longer came from the speakers. It seemed to be emitted by the walls, the air, her own skin.

'Stop!' she shouted. 'Whatever you are, stop! Leave me alone!' Another phrase, the same one she had used when she had first encountered Eqalussuaq, pressed at her. 'Not me!'

The scream stopped.

Lea waited. The calm felt like deafness. Tentatively, she plugged in the speakers and turned them on. Nothing.

Safe and sound.

With shaking hands, she booted the computer, then scrolled down to the first recordings of that final day in the sea. She selected the first file. A low, warm, creaking sound came from the speakers. The song of the iceberg had returned, pristine and ethereal, its wheezing groan continuing without interruption. No screaming, no anger.

She selected another recording made that same morning, then another. All were unimpaired, the clean, clear sounds matching the smooth waveforms on the screen.

Breathless, she gathered recordings together in the sound editor, overlaying and overlapping them, until the orchestra of soft moaning sounds grew into a single, overwhelming, glorious song. Bubbles rose around her. She felt warmth despite the chill. She danced slowly as if underwater.

Only one unwanted, alien sound penetrated through. Lea finally registered Peter's complaints from upstairs.

As she entered his bedroom, her son reached up blindly with both hands.

'It's okay,' Lea said, rocking him against her chest. 'It's gone.'

Peter said nothing. Tears trickled down his cheeks, making twin spots on her pyjamas. His open mouth worked from side to side. Lea remembered making the same motion herself, as the plane touched down and she tried to restore her hearing.

'Stop shouting,' Peter murmured.

Lea frowned. Was he dreaming?

But then he looked directly at her. His voice sounded far away. 'It hurts so much, Mum. Make it stop.'

She watched him writhe, his hands pressed against his ears

and his face pushed into the pillow. She felt a sudden certainty that it wouldn't help.

Peter's body was slack in her arms as she made her way downstairs. She stood holding him, before her computer, watching the undulating shapes of the waveforms on the screen. The iceberg recordings continued playing. Warm and heavenly.

She hesitated for several moments before laying Peter down on the battered studio sofa. Her hands wavered over the computer keyboard.

Peter's mouth contorted with pain, a thin white line pressed tight as if withholding something trying to force its way out.

It felt like a choice. Save the recordings, or Peter. Eqalussuaq was demanding that she choose.

She understood that her hesitation was unforgivable. She understood that she would spend her life attempting to rationalise the fact that she had even considered the alternative.

She looked at her son.

She chose.

14Sep16. Select all.

She wept a little.

Delete.

Peter whimpered as Lea smoothed his hair, then pressed his head further into the sofa cushion. His body shivered and shook. Clearly, he was still in agony.

She yanked out the plug to the computer and clawed at its case.

In the lean-to beyond the kitchen she found a hammer and chisel. As she cracked through the casing of the computer she shouted and wailed, a sound almost as feral as the scream on the recordings. The chisel revealed the internal hard drive, then fractured it. Once it was in pieces Lea turned her attention to the portable drives. In her desperation she shattered them all.

If anything, Peter appeared to be suffering even more now. His knees pulled up to his chin. As he rocked back and forth, his entire body spasmed.

Then his white lips trembled. They parted, showing his teeth.

The scream of whatever had followed Lea from the Arctic burst forth. Peter's head rattled from side to side with the effort of restraining himself against the force of the sound.

Lea gripped his hands. She pleaded.

But she understood. Destroying the recordings wasn't all that Eqalussuaq demanded.

'It's not him you want,' she said in a whisper. 'It's me.'

Peter's eyes opened.

Lea gripped the wooden arm of the sofa.

It hit her. Creaking limbs, something bellowing, screams that knifed through the water.

She clamped her hands over her ears, without any effect. The shriek took swipes at her head and torso, threatening to send her toppling. Her body convulsed with the cold.

Peter recovered within hours.

Lea's tinnitus would be permanent, the doctor said, though over time it transitioned from excruciating to deafening to a persistent, wavering drone.

She stood on the rock outcrop at dusk, facing out to sea. She watched a flock of gulls, concentrating on the shifting shapes that they formed, at first a ribbon, then a fat arrow, then a winding river.

She stretched her body upwards, tracking the flock, then winced at a pain in her stomach. She pulled her cardigan and T-shirt up. The thing had left her, but it had also left its mark. If it had ever been a real wound, one might have said it was healing fast. It was clear that the scar would remain, though, a single line of ripped, raw, pink flesh that corkscrewed around her abdomen.

A wave curled into existence and bundled itself towards the shore. Once she might have worn her binaural microphones to capture the sounds of the wind and waves, but the ringing in her ears interfered with the recordings. Now the sounds of the island served only as a temporary mask over the hisses and shrieks.

Above her, for a few seconds, the flock of birds formed a new shape, something sinewy and snub-nosed. It flexed and flicked its tail as it swam across the darkening sky.

Bight, Tomcat and the Moon.
Carmen Marcus

I'm me, Bight, I'm wearing my dad's old smock flecked with fish scales and white with salt lines. I'm barefoot on road dust. I'm thirteen and a girl, double bad luck if you're a fisherman but I'm not. I'm the keeper of the Last Sea on the road and it's time to rock the boat.

Moon's as full as she'll get since the Big Ebb, just a fish scale sliver, since humans went walking all over her face in their fat white boots, then probes to study her plumes. Enough's enough, so she cut her ties and drifted taking the sea with her. My father, a fisherman, caught the last of the sea, scooped her up, fish and all into the Seahouse. 'Stick to the roads,' he said, 'and steer clear of ghost currents.' So now I'm the moon to my finny friends, the tidal pull of my tiny sea until I find the true blue.

The Seahouse is two boats stuck together, one on top of the other like pursed wooden lips. The bottom-house is where the last of the fishes live. The top-house is where I live. I sleep over water so I always dream of floods. The Seahouse balances on an A-frame pulled by the tractor. Tonight I'm hanging from the starboard side shucking the Seahouse so it bounces on its big rubber tyres. Fish love moon-rock nights. The whelks tuck their spiny legs inside their shells and let themselves roll. The big monkfish totters on his tiny pectorals across the beam. The mackerels, well they're the first to go moon-mad, flashing their forked tails at the sky. I can hear the water slapping up the insides of the boat like a crowd going wild. As I swing up over the gunwale I see the anemones spurt their firework colours. Ha ha. Little punks.

I don't show the Sink folks this bit, moon-rock nights are just for us. But they are for show - my scaly, spiny underwater friends. Maybe I shuck too much tonight. I got a belly full of broken glass ache and three red blood spots drop onto the road dust between my feet. I can't get sick like my dad, I got promises to keep. So I stick to the old black roads like he said.

There it is - the smoking stack of a Sink. A wheezing twist of humans squatting round underground pools. Sinks don't have names or signposts. Proper names are for things that will last or be remembered. I roll up.

'Remember the days when there were still fish in the oceans and cars on the road?'

I give it a good lung holler over the tractor engine and clang the mast bell.

'Come see, come see - the one, the only, the wet, the weird, the Last Sea on the road.'

They used to pay when it still stung that the moon pulled away and the whole ocean buggered off down a crack in the Earth. But tonight, when I let them climb up the big treads of the wheels, they peer through the portholes and what they mostly feel is disappointed. They rub their coins in the red dust of their pockets and keep the water pots they promised for a look. Fish is fish, scales and gills. What more do they want? Mussels click. Urchins sting. 'So ugly,' they said, 'don't even make us hungry.' Well screw you. My friends aren't for eating.

The Sinkers like the saltwater battery best. It's just an old plastic box I use to test the water salinity like my dad showed me. Seawater is alive because of the salt. All the coloured bulbs light up like a birthday cake. 'Awww,' they go. But tonight only seven lights light. My water's dying and I don't know what I'm going to tell the fish. They flutter their gills at me just the same. I dunk my head under and I tell them so the Sinkers can't hear.

'I'm just a thirteen-year-old kid. I don't know shit about how to read the stars or get you home.'

Mickey Fin poofs his cool blue lips on my fingertip. Kiss. Kiss. There's a ripping inside of me, way past guilt. If this is it - current-struck - I've had it. Can't be, 'cos I never even seen so much as a dust twitch of a real ghost current. I pick Mickey up and get the battery and I push my way into the shouts and reaching hands wanting to touch the silver fish. They think this is some new show.

Inside the Sink reeks. Water's too precious for washing bodies in here. I swim everyday. I must smell like every summer holiday they ever had. Makes them go funny. 'Specially the men but I'm thirteen, pale and titless as the moon. I've tested Sink water before but there's very little life in it even though it's been through so many people. There's a wall of big blokes round the pool, ghouls mirrored in its wet eye, Clonks we call 'em, their blades are made from old garden spades and you don't want a clonk from one of them.

'Wait your turn.'

There's a mucky sort of order in the Sinks.

'Don't want to drink, I want to test. I've got fish. They could live in your Sink.'

'Don't want fish piss in my pool.'

Here's the Sink King now. So I show him Mickey Fin, who's got his wriggle on now he's sussed the air's too light to push through his gills. Sorry Mickey. The Sink King nods, curious and I dip my battery in. All the lights light up and of course I get an 'Awww' from the crowd. Their dust-raw eyes prick up at the pretty lights. Idiots. Then it's little Mickey's turn. I seen him grow from egg into the squiggles on his back, like I wrote my name on him. I seen him tickle his way out of Dora crab's black claw. He's a survivor. He's straight in, I don't see him, just the ripple he leaves behind. No one's breathed for a whole minute now. Then his silver half moon belly tips up in the black water. I wade in, slipping past the Clonks. He's not moving. Sorry-sorry-sorry Mickey. The Sink King's laughing and stoking his brazier for a fish supper. He tries to take Mickey right out of my hand. No way am I letting go. I kick the fire and the dust in the air sparks. The Clonks are busy trying to put out their King and I'm off.

I'm almost at the Seahouse, when these red fast hands snatch Mickey right out of mine.

'Give me back my fish!'

Mickey's so small, curled nose to tail on the pink pad of a paw. This bloke is a real ginger scruff, a cheeky Tomcat. I heard of Purrmen but never seen one close. I heard after the Big Ebb folk would eat anything, their own pets and worse. But the problem with cats is they got nine lives and at least seven came bursting back through the skins of those what ate them. Purrmen - whiskers and claws and triangles for ears.

'Where you heading in that?' he says, whistling at the Seahouse through a smile full of pins.

'The sea,' I say.

'You won't get there by road. You know your stars?'

This is a bone of contention as my dad was supposed to show me how to sail by the stars. He said he'd teach me when I was older. I got older. He didn't. He got taken by a ghost current, struck so bad he looped a knot around his own neck just to keep his water still.

There's a loud angry noise coming from the Sink. I rev up

the tractor.

'Take me with you,' he meowls, a cool rumble that hushes my bellyache, 'And I'll teach you your stars.'

He climbs up, Mickey still coiled on his palm, and I don't stop him, but I make sure this cat knows:

'Mickey's not for eating.'

Inside the bottom-house the Purrman looks less ginger. He's got poor little Mickey by the tail, dunking him in the water but Mickey's silver's coming back. Mickey pulls himself free and sulks, hiding in the dead-man's-fingers.

'What's your name?'

'Tomcat,' I have to laugh. 'What's yours?'

'Bight.'

'What? Bite like bit?' He snaps his teeth closed, a perfect fit. 'What kind of name is that for a girl?'

'It's my name. It's the bend in a rope before you make the knot. It's the beginning.' That's what my dad told me. It's still a rubbish name for a girl. My mum didn't get a say as she died having me. Dad kept her magazines so's I'd learn how to be a proper lady but how's a girl called Bight supposed to cascade? Tomcat looks in my sea just to see himself, checking out his ginger whiskers. Dora crab's a soft-shelled tart, she blows him love bubbles but he don't even blink.

'What d'you know about the sea?'

'You don't do much small talk do you?'

I keep quiet long enough to prove his point. He takes off his shirt. I get my knife.

'Steady,' he says 'cos he wants me to see his scars. 'You heard of ghost currents? That's where I got these.'

'Heard enough to steer clear.'

'Well we won't find the Lost Sea on the road. Look up.'

He tilts my head to the sky.

'That's the North Star. The stillest point in the sky. Stick out your arms.'

He gets behind me, resting his chin on my neck and I can feel the rolling instrument of his purr under his fur.

'Your right hand is east, your left west. Keep watching the star.'

He spins me round so his words fill the tickle cup under my chin.

'We're going south.'

I daren't look down, the star is the only part of me that's still.

My bellyache's gone. Moon's as round and black as Tomcat's eyes. He's cleaning his whiskers like he's ready to eat, grinning at the old magazine pictures of women on my walls.

'What you got these for? You like girls?.'

I punch his arm. I can't explain these women - their quiet lips, the heavy swells of their woman's bits under silk. I look for them in my hurting body certain they will never come. I seen this world curling up in knots to die and me - I'll be stuck at bad-luck thirteen forever. I draw my mother's empty make-up brush across my cheek and my eyes light up like the saltwater battery. I always wanted a ginger Tom to curl up on my lap and to rub the red velvet of his ears.

I find Dora Crab's lonely black claw in Tomcat's bed. I throw it at him and he catches it and slowly blinks his eyes leaning into a kiss.

'It's my nature,' he says.

'It's my boat,' I says and lose my fingers in his fur to push him over board.

Then we hit something - the big old bones of a wreck. I pull on my mother's old silk skirt, up over the bare angles of my hips and it shines like I'm walking in water. For the first time I feel the soft pinch and sink of sand under my feet, between my toes. A stray wind rasps it against my bare legs like a cat's tongue. I take a handful in my pocket for the fish. There's no sign of Tomcat.

The wreck is nothing like the Seahouse, dried up Mermaid's purses still cling to her, clams guard her crumbling belly. I see she's got a name 'Queenie', like a girl-cat. The sand bed swirls and lifts me off my feet - ghost current. Up I go and then it throws me against the wreck. Tomcat's there, he catches me tearing my mother's skirt, his fingers curl around my ribs.

'I've got you kid.'

But the current's got us both, spinning us in the muscle of its memory. I take Tomcat's shoulder and we could be dancing in the roll of the ghost sea. Death. That's what I'm thinking as I tipple topple into Tomcat's blue eyes. There's the sea and he's had it all this time, locked up frozen in the ice flecks of his eyes.

'Let me go,' I tell him as he topples me and I hook my heel around his foot, forgetting how easy it is to hold onto something that doesn't have scales. But the current rips me - 'Aiyee' - and lickety-splits me to pieces.

'You got properly current struck kid.' I'm shucked up all right, my head is empty, dark and tumbling, not a twitch of a still star in my head. I can feel the ghost of his long claw on my ribs, bruising. It's a good deep-down grown-up kind of hurt that I need cool water to fix. I drop into the bottom-house and they scatter, like they can taste it on me. The memory of their water. They nip at the bruises blooming on my ribs with questions I can't answer and I wonder how Tomcat really got his scars.

'Throw him overboard,' they say, Dora tapping her one good claw. I can't tell that them we need him because I've lost my still-north.

I dream of floods and wake up with sand in the creases of my sheets.

We roll further south and still no sign of sea, just the abyssal plain stretched out like a warm cat. The moon spins, turning her face round, fuller than I've ever seen her. My bellyache's back and wakes me up. Rock the boat time no matter what. I hold onto the gunwale and shuck until my knuckles are white. Only Mickey Fin's riding the sweep 'cos no one else feels like bouncing. I slip into the bottom-house while the waves are still pulsing.

'Come on,' I say but the mussels don't click and I can taste their quiet death. Monkfish sulks at the bottom and Dora looks like she's ready to be eaten. They float so still, so unlike the red current running through me.

'Dad,' I said, like he wasn't dust, and I picture his big hands looping the first knot in the rope. 'You shouldn't never have called me Bight.' And now I know it, I cut my own red rope and jump in mixing my water up with the Last Sea, salt-water filling up my nose.

Tomcat's face floats above me, a second moon. He has me by my silk skirt. His white teeth flash and he pushes his own breath into me, whiskery prickles around my lips. He tips me over his knee and slaps my back. I'm so mad he's made me begin again I push him in the deep end and he yowls. He can't swim. His eyes - blue, black - flicker as his lungs panic and gulp wingfulls of water. So I haul him up and punch his ribs for Dora as he coughs up.

'Trust me,' he says.

'Ha,' I say, then shut up 'cos I hear this 'Shush shush'. I've never heard it before it's like the earth breathing.

On the horizon the red head of the sun crests, setting fire to an impossible blue line. I put on my mother's silk dress for this, ready to meet the sea, the red sun pressing on our backs. But the sea is trapped, a steep canyon lies between us. There are a thousand lights moving up towards us from the drop. A tusky Purrman is the first to arrive, grey as dust, he slaps his paw around Tomcat and murowhs his hellos. The big old Grey-stripe thumps his paw on my boat. Dora crab keeps quiet. Grey-stripe wears a coat of mackerel skin and a crown of mussel shells. He shines like the sea on the horizon. My finned friends know the moon is full but they are still as they have ever been. They must taste their dead even through the wood.

'Good work Tomcat, I'll give you five hundred for the boat.'

'Five? You haven't seen the fish yet, that's the Last Sea you're looking at there, there's whelk and…'

'And three hundred for the girl.'

My lips pop pop at the air like I'm still drowning, drawing at the nothing where water should be. Tomcat nods and smiles, triangles for ears and a kiss full of pins. It is his nature. But I'm Bight, I'm the bend, I'm the beginning, I'm double bad luck. I am the bloody moon. I shuck, running from one side of the bottom-house to the other. Those with legs run with me. The water lapping up and over the sides shouting 'Shush' to the other water sitting quiet at the horizon. I can feel the pull right under my ribs where my dreams of floods come from. The fist of the returning sea smashes the bottom-house open. Wraps its wet paw around Tomcat who is blowing kisses, his last, to me. I see my ocean come and pull him by his ginger tail.

The fish keep me alive and well in the upside down top-house wrapped in a pocket of air. They promise me one day they will find land. I dream of cat's claws and my father's hands. These live currents wash away the memory of dust. Mickey asks me if I remember:

'The days long ago when there were still fish on the roads and dust for sea, there lived a young woman who would rock the boat.'

He calls his friends to come and see the show. Clown fish bring him pearls to swim in my white hair. But he cannot make the water still on dark moon nights for me.

The King Tide
Alex Reece Abbott

Anne couldn't resist the glint that called from the dark mussel-studded rocks.

Ehura eased the find from the leathery bull-kelp fingers, rinsed the bottle in the sea, and handed it to her.

It was unsealed, and a tiny chip on the rim scratched rough against Anne's skin, but otherwise the glass had been delivered intact, one day before the king tide. She pushed back her straw bonnet and tilted the bottle till it drained, water hissing on the grey boulders. She licked her lips and tasted brine.

She ran her fingers along the narrow neck and over the soft roll of the pig-snout lip. Like a genie's bottle, her deep sea treasure formed beneath the waves. Holding it up to the sun, she wondered if it had come from the hell-hole town far across the bay.

Ehura called out, then headed off in the direction of a pair of bandy, jet black birds that were patrolling the outgoing tide.

Daydreams broken, Anne bustled to catch her up.

With a murmur of pleasure, the girl scanned the shoreline, flax kit swinging by her side. She gave a nod and came to an abrupt halt, then hitched her dress up into her drawers. Since there were no neighbours to gawp, Anne didn't bother to chide her.

Without hesitation, Ehura waded in until the water washed

around her strong brown calves. As the next wave retreated, she studied an arrowhead of air bubbles puncturing the sand.

She prowled into the middle of the patch like a stalking cat. The evicted oystercatcher and her restless mate trotted on up the beach, occasionally pausing to probe a promising new patch with their long crimson bills. Ehura patiently worked her way along the bank of shellfish in a shuffling dance. Screwing her feet into the soft wet sand, she broke up the bed with her toes, never losing her balance.

Bent double, she scrabbled and rose with a handful of fat squirting pipis.

She squealed, wiping her salty face on her sleeve. After rinsing the shellfish in the waves, she broke one open and offered it to Anne.

Anne shook her head. She would wait, steam the shellfish… perhaps serve them with a little vinegar and onion, and some slabs of soda bread.

Ehura was already scooping the creamy meat straight from another shell, swallowing it raw as an oyster. Catching sight of Anne removing her boots and tucking the hem of her skirt into her apron, she chuckled.

As the women bowed down, digging side by side, the oystercatchers' shrill complaints echoed around the cove.

When the flax kit was full, Anne washed her hands in the clear sea. Each finger was tipped with a dark gritty crescent of stubborn sand, packed tight against her pink skin. It struck her that hunting for pipis was like searching for her faith: sometimes, if she reached out, she sensed the possibility of something, out of sight but real. Yet, like the burrowing molluscs, whenever she chased, it edged away.

Ehura carried the bulging kete with ease, singing one of her songs all the way back to the house. There'd be no shellfish yet:

Anne had learned that lesson the hard way. Ehura would have to soak them overnight. In the shade of the lean-to kitchen, in an old pan of fresh seawater, the pipis would spit their grit. They'd be ready to cook tomorrow. Tonight it would be cold mutton, relish and some vegetables from the garden.

Again.

Down on the beach, a family of raucous herring gulls squawked and squabbled over the remains of a dead snapper, washed in on the morning surf. Anne turned her mind to her new treasure, and that far more pleasant subject preoccupied her as they picked their way along the rippled golden sand. By the time they reached the kitchen, the bottle had already dried in the stifling summer breeze.

Anne left Ehura to clean their harvest, the girl still grinning at the size of their catch.

After searching for a place to display her find, she settled on the parlour mantel where the late morning sun caught the glass, sending shimmers of myrtle green across the plain wall. The bottle could stay for a day. No harm done.

It held no letter, yet it carried a message: some sacred connection that stretched beyond the isolated mission station where they'd been settled for five long years. Over sixty months and not a single convert.

Yet.

This bay, at the rugged northern tip of New Zealand, was a sharp, sometimes bitter, contrast to the sentimental scenes that decorated their white and blue tea-set. That was all wild roses, and idyllic English country churches, prosperous villages and calm, far-off meadows, like William's Oxfordshire.

She owned no fine china: her set was all mass-produced seconds, befitting lay missionaries. A good enough show of civilisation to grease social relations with any visitors who made the trek to see them.

To see William.

Her conscience prickled.

William.

William, who would deem the bottle frivolous and a bad example for the natives.

William, who only ever allowed them a dose of spirits to help them out of their sickness.

There were plenty of stories about the whalers taking their shore leave across the bay, full of rum and riot after two years at sea. He certainly wouldn't entertain the notion that a genie's bottle could grant a wish… no, they had prayer.

Prayer. Sent to the bay to do God's work and left to live on the same allowance as a Parramatta convict. Forgive me, she said out loud, not that there was anyone to understand her.

At sunrise, William had set off up their dirt track on more urgent business for the parson. And, even if he had been at home, it would be unmanly for her husband to listen to her prattling. Still, she wondered about an alternative means of being heard. Short rations and unreliable supplies were probably taking their toll, that was all.

She told herself so, again and again.

And then, there's the loneliness.

The bottle could stay until William returned.

There could be no harm.

That evening, after prayers, when Ehura and the children were sleeping, and the servant girls were bedded down, Anne caught sight of herself in the mirror.

She made herself smile. Although her face was already well-lined, it shone with a serenity that William claimed to envy. The ribbons of her lace bonnet were tied firmly under a determined chin. Her hair, swept back from a centre-part, framed her like a pair of salt and pepper curtains these days.

She was sturdy, slightly taller than William; good Viking stock from a long line of Swedes and Danish sailors and traders, so her father liked to joke.

She studied her reflection, letting herself wonder how her family and friends had aged. She pulled away. Pointless to dwell, since she'd probably never see any of them again.

Lying in her four-poster bed, her smile returned at the thought of her new treasure until she remembered that keeping it for good would be impossible. Not only because of William, there was the outcry if the parson should see it… unthinkable.

Or worse, her neighbour, Mrs Cowan, visiting and bringing airs and graces with her gossip.

Anne could already see her, pacing in the parlour and pretending to study the sampler above the mantelpiece. Stitched during their voyage from Port Jackson, William had made a frame for her handiwork from some of the local kauri wood.

"Preach the Gospel to Every Creature."
Anne Bell, CMS, 1814.

The sampler was Anne's useful example to the girls she taught. Even though the once vibrant threads had already been bleached and faded by the sun, she was confident that her neighbour's judgemental eye could find no fault with the needlework.

Mrs Cowan always started by clearing her throat. 'Ahem. And have you been quite well Mrs Bell?'

Anne would smile and exchange pleasantries, as she did every visit, although it always felt more akin to a military manoeuvre than any dance of etiquette. 'We enjoy our health. I find the climate here is generally fine and healthy and agrees with my constitution. We are in quite good spirits.'

This time, when Mrs Cowan nods towards the mantelpiece, Anne will know that it's not the needlework catching her gimlet eye.

'You have yourself a bottle I see,' Mrs Cowan will say, smug and determined as their pup Elijah when he's digging up an especially tasty morsel in the yard.

Anne will hold her ground, look her in the eye. Tell her that it washed up in the morning tide. 'Pretty isn't it?'

She will hem and haw and chew her rubbery bottom lip. 'Is it not a… rum… bottle, Mrs Bell?'

And, Anne's demeanour will be a model of innocence. 'Is it? Perhaps once it was so. I am thinking I'll find some further purpose for it as a useful container…'

Mrs Cowan will suck her teeth and Anne will await her impending sermon. Back in the Parramatta days, how often the parson had blasted them from the pulpit about rum being the scourge of the colony, one which had often produced jealousies and misunderstandings. The barter of spirits had long been a Serious Evil in the Settlement of Port Jackson; Anne cannot argue this.

'The source of many unhappy differences,' Anne will offer, even though William believes that the smallest drop, if required, can be medicinal.

'Quite so,' Mrs Cowan will murmur.

No doubt, the dog-with-a-bone will want to know one thing: was it full of spirits when Anne had found it? Mrs Cowan's pinched face always lets Anne know that any answer she could conjure up will be unsuitable.

She'll explain that she came across the bottle among the rocks as they were gathering pipis.

And, Mrs Cowan will grimace, then make some comment

about horrid, gritty little things and no doubt, blame Mr Cowan for making her eat the shellfish. 'My husband insisted on serving them once, after eating them at some village feast somewhere down the coast. Chewing some of your husband's old rope that he makes with the natives would be more pleasant and probably more nutritious, Mrs Bell.'

Then she'll bray like a donkey at her joke. 'Suitable only for bait. Or the natives of course. Would you eat them, Mrs Bell, truly?'

And, the usual silence would stretch out between them.

Respect for your elders or not, Mrs Cowan was a busy-body.

Still, she was company of a sort. And she spoke English.

Anne shuddered and drew her covers around her like a shield.

Eyes closed tight, she recalled her own arrival. Had she ever felt so bitter or frightened back then? She was no longer sure that she remembered.

And, life before that day had faded to a pleasing dream.

When they'd landed in the bay, three other families had joined them for a while, but they'd soon returned. Since then, her life had seemed charted for certain: the youngest wife and the only woman who would stay for the rest of her life.

But the bottle, that could not stay.

Although, with favourable currents and tides, it might sail faster than the ships that took one hundred weeks to carry their mail to London. Perhaps, some kind soul might even intercept her bottle, and hasten its journey home.

She wondered what message she could send out into the world from this dismal valley. In the beginning God created…

In the beginning…

In the…

As she lay waiting for sleep to come, Anne relived the ripples of excitement from that morning, when she'd first spied her treasure nestling among the rocks.

She yawned and felt better than she had since the day they landed in the cove.

She finally drifted off, dreaming that she was a ship, safe inside deep green glass, sailing back to England, home to her old, easier life.

The next morning, she rose with the dawn for the king tide.

She admired her bottle in the parlour for a while, before taking the pipi-shell path into the scrub-framed garden. The chickens clucked around her feet, hungry disciples pressing to be fed. She sang and her sheep choir bleated their response, and she sang on: to them and anyone else who might hear her hymn.

After breakfast, Anne took Ehura down to her favourite tree near the shore. They settled on an old crate with their needle-work, making the most of the breeze and the light.

The waves lapped high on the beach, higher than they would ever reach until next winter, when once again the sun and the moon would slide into perfect alignment. She gave silent thanks to the waves for what she had received.

She glanced over at Ehura; her stitching lay on her lap. The sharp-eyed girl was staring, one eyebrow raised at a dust-cloud rising on the ridge. They were not expecting anyone and William was not due for at least another week. Then again Anne seldom knew when visitors might appear at their door, or how many.

She watched until Ehura took up her sewing once more, both satisfied that it was only the breeze.

A soaring albatross cackled and Anne searched the sky. As she found him gliding effortlessly out to his home at sea, she felt certain that the Lord was on her side.

Her decision was made.

William might mind her find, but truly, he need never know about it or its purpose. She would write out her wish, neat and careful as she taught Ehura and the girls, then seal it in the rescued rum bottle with a cork and a good smear of candle wax.

No matter who came down that dirt-track that morning, she would take her message down to the waves and set it free. Perhaps it was wrong to place her faith in the king tide, but it was not as if she had anything more to lose.

From that day she studied the sea, the turquoise sea that had brought her to the bay, the sea that had delivered her find, the sea that had taken her family and friends away; the sea that would claim several of her children.

Morning and night, she scoured the shoreline to see what answers, what fortune the sea might have delivered.

And she waited; waited for the king tide to come around again.

Fillet
Liz Wride

The tail-end of the week meant Fish Supper Friday, and Phil's was delivered rotten, and right on cue. Spewing through his letterbox were tentacles, scales, and stick-in-your-throat bones. The stench began to sink into the wallpaper.

He struggled stoically with the still-squirming, if lifeless squid. He made sure the gunk got under his nails. He made sure that he'd smell the salty blood of the sea, the tenth time he washed his hands. It was only at the very last, that he seemed to be wrestling a Kraken. It was only at the very last, that the steely jaws of the letterbox snapped shut. It was only at the very last, Phil was greeted with clean-cut chunks of tentacle, in a dark, inky sauce.

His fast fish food delivery had caused such a commotion, he hadn't noticed the familiar hissing sound. But he heard it now. Then there was a pause, followed by a violent shaking of a can, the sort that had ball bearings inside, to mix up the contents.

It didn't matter how many times he'd painted the front of the house…

He didn't even have to go outside and look.

He knew what they'd sprayed:

'Fillet.'

'Think fish, think Phil's Fillets.'

It was his market stall's unofficial moto – back when he could show his face in the community. Second stall on the left, follow your nose and the smell of saltwater. He'd sold everything: plaice, mackerel, Dover sole, wild sea bass tail, tuna steaks, monster crab claws, scallops, whole prawns, cockles, squid, whole cod - some glass-eyed, all gleaming.

'A salmon fillet, please, Phil. Nice and pink for our Sophie's christening.'

When you bagged the fish, you had to stick the label on it in one fluid movement, press down hard with the palm of your hand, seal of approval, almost.

'Laverbread, please Phil. Going to have some tonight with bacon… all mixed up in the pan… lovely… maybe put some mushrooms in…'

There had been something for Phil in the familiarity of their footsteps, the community. The pensioners who got off the bus the same time every day and traded 'big fish' stories from their childhood rock-pooling days, as they waited for their boil-in-the-bag kippers.

Or the teenagers, who spoke out from underneath their hoodies: 'Is it true oysters make you…?'

'Brainy?' Phil had said. 'Packed full of zinc if you're revising for your exams…' Most of the boys had gone, scarpered. One was left, shuffling his feet. As he stretched out his hand, Phil saw the scribbles of school work: 'Read pages 20 – 50' written on the back of his hand.

'Can I get some of those…?' He'd mumbled.

But like the teenagers, most of the market's customers were long gone. The Friday fish supper had given way to TV dinners; and 'Half a pound of prawns' had become, 'Sorry, I'm allergic to shellfish'.

Sure, back then, he could have packed it all in, folded up his tarpaulin once and for all, gone to work in a supermarket chain, where he'd wear a name badge… Or he could make his market stall great again, put it on the map.

There'd always been stories. They were passed on by the seashells, as children held them to their ears to hear the sea. They'd run back to their parents, saying they'd heard the sound of waves, but really, they'd heard the roar of the ocean, the deep-down blackness, where things with no eyes lived…

'The Kraken, The Kraken, The Kraken. Squeeze the life out of you, it will…'

'There are mermaids in the shallows. They drag you down into the depths. You'll be married to the sea, then…'

'The Gulper eels will swallow you whole…'

'The Ghost sharks will sneak up on you…'

'The Giant spider crabs that will crawl all over you….'

As Phil approached the shore, he'd already decided what supermarket he'd work at, decided what colours he'd liked best. It wouldn't be so bad. People attended supermarkets like clockwork, after work at 5pm, at 10am on a Sunday: he'd get his community back. But then there was that feint glimmer in the distance, the hope that he could turn that market stall around.

It was the hope that killed him the most.

He cast his line.

This was the importance of fishing, something people who never did it didn't understand. There was a point when Phil had been standing there so long he'd ceased to be. There was no barrier between him and the wave. Now, he wasn't hooking the fish, he wasn't fishing, they would seek him out.

It was the hope that killed him the most.

He was still aware of the incoming tide, the increasing saltiness of the air, the lightness of his line.

The people didn't come to him.

The fish didn't come to him.

It was the hope that killed him the most.

He was still aware of the incoming tide, and the sudden, incredible weight at the end of his line. His eyes grew wide. This was the massive fish, the stuff of palms-apart, 'this big' monster catch stories. He began to reel it in but the line snapped.

It was the hope that killed him the most.

There was a splash, and a silvery flash of a tail.

His line had snapped clean in half. The hook, the bait, gone. That had been some big fish, alright. If nothing else, he'd be the only supermarket fish monger to have his own 'big fish' story.

'What the hell…'

In the near distance, a thin arm, reaching up through the suddenly stirring water. His mind had been playing tricks, the reflections of the water. There was no tail. This was flotsam and jetsam, a discarded shop mannequin, that had found its way into the ocean, rather than the landfill.

Then the arm moved. Something shop mannequins are never normally able to do.

'Oh, shit…'

A swimmer had got caught up in his line, probably someone training for a triathlon. She probably had his hook embedded in her side. This was a big fish story, all right…

He rushed out, half-walking, then wading, then nearly swimming. His thoughts crashed against the inside of his skull. He tried to remember first aid training, a must for anyone who spent as much time as he did around fillet knives. A, B, C. Airway… He pulled at the arm, bringing a young girl to the surface. She was stripped to the waist, her long hair hanging limp and dark like straggles of seaweed, her skin so translucent he could see the thin lines of her veins like a map. Her eyes were closed, her breathing barely there. He feared, amid the shifting sand and the swirling water, that he had gone and killed a swimmer. Knowing his luck, she was probably an Olympic hopeful too. Instead of imprisonment he'd be weighed down with what would have been her gold medal, before they pushed him off a cliff into the depths of the ocean.

He shook her gently.

'Come on, wake up. Come on. Come on!'

He shook her again.

'I'll go and get help. I'll call the coastguard. My phone's in my pocket…'

Her eyes opened. For a moment, Phil saw colours in her iris that didn't seem to exist anywhere else on Earth. It was the iridescence of shells or scales, but it was fleeting. Suddenly her eyes were nothing more than the creamy white gleam of pearls. She was as blind as the half-formed, nightmarish things from the depths.

He could feel his heart race, now. The primal sort of panic no first aid class could train out of you. She would be all right. He'd carry her to the shore. He'd put her on the beach. He'd do CPR. She would be all right.

It was the hope that killed him the most.

He tried to pick her up He expected to hook his hand under her knees, and lift her out of the water, except he didn't feel skin, he felt scales. They were thick and rough, like the skin of a huge salmon.

It couldn't be…

These were the stuff of legend, of children's storybooks and 'big fish' stories.

It could be, and it was.

They drag you down into the depths…you'll be married to the sea, then…

As he tried to lift her out of the water, he noticed the gaping wound across her stomach, just above where flesh met fish. From her wound, poured the blood of the sea: a clear, salty water.

'You'll be all right…' he said.

Did she even understand?

Or did her language operate like the low sonar song of whales?

He'd lift her out of the water, take her to hospital. Did the NHS deal with animals? Technically it was the human half of her that was injured. Maybe he should take her to the vet? Or the sea-life centre an hour's drive away…

But he couldn't lift her.

It was as if she had been harpooned by Poseidon's trident.

Could she even breath the air? Was he slowly killing her?

He let go, and she sank beneath the choppy water.

He expected her to rise again, but her body stayed there, stuck on whatever had slashed her across the belly. In the shallows there was nothing but Phil and a very real, very dead, mermaid.

Phil had been staring into the abyss.

He hadn't bothered to go and check the graffiti that marked the front of his house. He knew it would still be blood-wet. He'd been washing his hands, turning the council-approved tap water inky-black. The stuff that came out of the taps was a million miles away from the ocean. It had been through the system, treated and filtered so much, it was nearly unnatural. It was nothing like the rambunctiousness of sea water. The only water that didn't quench thirst. The only water, that if you swallowed it, seemed to fill you up, seemed to drag you down…

He pulled the plug and watched the black drain away… but it wasn't gone… because the darkness was inside him…

Phil should have walked away, waded away, swam away, ventured back to the shore, but his brain seemed flooded with salt water. All his humanity seemed to leave him, like flotsam and jetsam, drifting into the distance.

He had caught a fish. A really big fish.

The fishermen in the North Sea, catching net-full after net-full, didn't feel remorse for the gasping fish that hit their decks. He hadn't felt bad any other time he'd gone fishing. He'd just felt relaxed, the worries of the market stall drowning slowly.

He took the knife he always carried in his pocket.

All he was doing was filleting a freshly-caught fish.

The meat was tough, and Phil hacked away at it, with the sharp, blade. He was glad that mythical creatures didn't bleed red, otherwise, animal campaigners would have appeared out of nowhere, bobbing in dinghies, shouting at him through megaphones. When he carried it home, it would just look like he was carrying a huge tuna.

Nobody felt remorse over tuna.

His arm around her waist, her naked breasts pressing against his chest, he cut across, just below her belly button, in swift skillful strokes. Slowly, he separated flesh from fish. He was supporting the tail now, hoping it wouldn't get away. It seemed free from whatever had been holding it down.

There was only an inch or so to go. Soon, he would have cut all the way across and this half-girl could get married to the sea, be taken as Davey Jones' wife.

As the blade moved and severed the last piece of mermaid-tail, the girl gasped, as if given the kiss of life by some invisible force. Her skin seemed to flush with all the pink of oxygenated blood. The blinding cloud lifted from her eyes, and her hair hung, aqua-tinged around her face. Her chest rose and fell, in short, stunted, breaths; like someone who had just been plunged into the ocean and was going into cold-water shock.

Phil felt his stomach churn. And he was a man with strong sea legs.

He was still holding onto what was left of her waist.

'I'll, I'll take you… the vet… the doctor…. stitches…'

He felt the tears roll down his cheeks: a different kind of saltwater.

Her eyes were a deep violet, and wide with panic. She saw him. Really saw him.

'I'll… I'll…' He glanced down. There was blood on his knife. Red blood.

She should have been full of the blood of the sea.

He had turned the entire sea red, and it raged around them.

Suddenly, he felt her go rigid, the gasping breaths stopped.

She was bloodlessly pale and translucent once more.

The tail of meat was bigger than any fish Phil had ever seen. In his kitchen, he filleted in the usual way. He made sure he didn't cut against the grain, so that it would cook tender. He kept the iridescent tail fin. That would have pride of place on the ice, in the middle of his market stall.

He closed the refrigerator door on the fish, so it chilled. Before he rinsed off his fillet knife, he saw a tiny piece of pink fish on the edge of the blade. He scooped it off the steel and popped it in his mouth.

He went into the bathroom to scrub his hands. The strip-light above him faltered. As it flickered back to life, he saw the monstrosity of his reflection. His eyes looked like blind hollows, barnacles stuck to his skin. One of his ears was nearly fully seashell, and from his chin extended a dark, tentacle beard. Taking on a life of their own, they coiled and recoiled, reaching for the mirror. His smile had turned sailor, teeth rotting, apart from the odd gold molar; and his breath was 100% proof: spiced rum. The gnarled leg of a giant spider crab appeared behind his ear as the crustacean climbed up the back of his neck.

He opened his mouth to scream, but the noise that came out was the roar of waves crashing against rocks: the sonar lament of the 52-hertz whale.

The light faltered again, and Phil once again regarded his own, weathered face in the bathroom mirror. He pulled at the skin under his eyes, revealing a slice of oxygenated red. He was human. He wasn't oceanic. He was just a fishmonger. He was just a good old fishmonger on a failing market stall.

His stomach churned like the sea.

As he vomited into the sink, he saw that he was bringing up nothing but salt water.

The people were three-deep in front of Phil's stall.

The word had spread, like the stories the seashells whispered in people's ears.

'Better than the tuna you get from the supermarket, and that stuff is from the extra-fancy-super-duper-posh-range…'

'Freshly caught, I heard…'

'The best sushi you'll ever taste…'

'I don't know, at my age, I like my fish cooked and battered…'

The customers marvelled at the rainbow sheen on the scales. They commented on the pink colour of the fish.

What was the best way to cook it?

Would it freeze?

One woman was feeding it to her cat: the most spoiled cat in the whole town.

Phil was met by a sea of green as people handed him fistfuls of notes.

When would he being having more in?

Then, he faced his final question – asked to him by a teenage boy, from underneath the heavy fabric of his hoodie. Without meeting Phil's eyes, the boy mumbled:

'Was it ethically sourced?'

The video of Phil cutting the mermaid clean in half, was online within hours.

The tagline read: 'You won't believe what this man does to this mermaid!'

Some called it click-bait, said you'd virus your computer if you opened the file. Others called it fake news and said it was all clever video editing.

But oyster-boy, the one with the school-notes scribbled on his hand, knew the truth. He'd filmed it all in HD. He'd seen Phil leave the girl for dead. He'd gone half-swimming, half-running into the blood-red water after Phil had left, but the girl was gone, nothing but sea foam.

Harris
Pauline Jérémie

A storm hits the island again during the night and three more men wash up on the beach. In the early hours of dawn they lie face down in the sand, their uniforms heavy and dark with water, seaweed in their hair and dried salt on the swollen skin of their hands. The wooden remains of their ship surround their bodies. Their eyes, open and glossy, reflect the warm colours of the morning sky as the sun rises and we start descending upon the beach.

We wear our traditional dresses, as always, red with chrysanthemums embroidered on the bottom hem, and carry fresh eggs in the pockets of our white aprons. Our feet dig into the sand wet with dew and the memory of tide as we approach the bodies, leaving a path of shallow holes behind us and the hair that escapes our bonnets is whipped back into our faces by the cutting sea wind. We do not talk when we kneel by the men, nor when we flip the bodies around and uncover the faces of loved ones and strangers - we do not talk any more at all.

The men are young as always. The water has left their skin tight and smooth as newborns'. The seashells in their hair look like ceramic hairpins, and here and there a brave crab walks across a still chest and disappears into the fold of a pocket. We gather around each body in silence, grab legs and arms, and carry them like bags of dirty sheets back up the hill and to the road where we haul them onto dark wooden carts. We arrange the bodies so that the faces are illuminated by the sun and place an egg in each of their hands. If the eggs break, the men will be buried; if not, their bodies will be burnt. We have started to run out of space in the town's graveyard.

The sun finishes rising as we pull the carts through the empty land, past fallen trees and battered fields, in the smell of salt and death and under a salmon-coloured sky. We know this path well, now. It was once the road to afternoons of bathing in freezing water with our mothers and fathers, running into waves and crashing onto the shore with them. Now we have become the mothers, and the fathers have all died, and the children do not go near the sea any more. Our convoy is silent as we march past cows and sheep on their morning graze, the hands of the dead lolling from the edges of their beds.

We reach the town as our people wake up to honour yet another arrival. Neighbours and friends and relatives stick their heads out of windows and doors to observe us as we walk down the main road. Children are held back by women young enough to be their sisters, and only a few old men show their faces. The young ones have all died and the old are dying and the smell of death is stronger here. A woman gasps and clutches her heart when she sees one of the men, but her cheeks remains dry and blank. The sea has swallowed all the tears we had to shed.

By the time we reach the cemetery the sun is up and shines onto our skins wet with sweat. We arrange the carts in a clean row in front of the gate and check the eggs. One of them broke in the palest man's cold hand, the yolk running through the stiff fingers like thick syrup, so some of us gather around him to pull his cart away from the others. We wheel the remaining men to our house in the island wind, our dresses flapping into our legs.

We remove our shoes and hang up our aprons at the door,

bring in fresh chrysanthemums in glass vases, and light candles to remove the smell of death, bitter and pungent, from our curtains and clothes. The men are lain onto kitchen tables covered with white sheets, their faces up and their eyes staring at the ceiling. We bring forward buckets of boiled water and clean cloths. Starting with their shoes, we undress the men, open their shirts, cut off their trousers. Our trained hands roam the swollen skin like ants, and we wash the bodies with the care of mothers and the gentleness of lovers. The dead men's faces glisten in the light of the candles, every pore, every hair, every wasted scar heightened, and the dancing flames cast shadows in every crook.

We have forgotten how it feels to touch warmth and life and so, as we wipe the sand and salt off nails and stomachs and legs, we ache to remember the movement of a rising chest, the beating of a heart in the wrist, the blinking of an eye; we imagine the distant echo of a familiar laugh, the feeling of a steady hand on the neck, the sensation of lips touching lips. When finally the manly smell of sweat comes floating back to us like a memory made of dust, we open the window and the scent of the nearby fire seeps into the room and breaks the fantasy. We close the men's eyes.

We bury them in the evening in the light of our torches and the set of the sun. The land has dried from the storm, but our shovels still crack the earth without effort, and so we dig holes long enough for the bodies to fit in, deep enough for their spirits not to come back. The ground is musky and moist; we dig up worms, cut in half.

No one attends the funerals any more, so we stand alone in the vastness of the land we are filling up with men, like seeds that will grow into nothing. We lay down stones where the dead lie and put out our torches in the soil. The wind picks up again as we leave the cemetery, and another storm hits the island during the night.

When It Sleets
Sarah Leavesley

'In Bath, England, in 1894, it rained jellyfish. In Tasmania, Australia, in 1996, it rained jellyfish. It's not known exactly how this happens. The most likely theory is that jellyfish live in the sky, trying to protect the earth from alien attack. Once every hundred years or so, a smack of sky-jellyfish tire and collapse.' Jellyfish Review

Historians called the phenomenon 'rain', but in eye-witness accounts it sounds more like a dirty sleet of dead mesoglea: slimy, sticky, slug-trailish. For days, Earth was covered in a thick glistening: trees, homes, streets trapped exactly as they were at that moment; lovers caught mid-kiss; dogs' jaws open, sharp teeth suspended mid-howl.

Once this tacky layer finally melted, people disentangled themselves in a dazed way, muscles aching. With nothing left to test, scientists couldn't fathom exactly what had happened. Or where and why the glooplasma layer had finally gone. Some theorised that a growing sycamore-twig might have burst the surface, prompting its disintegration. But melting didn't really cover its complete disappearance, the lack of even particles or gas traces in the air.

Still, several religious leaders heralded the jellyfish as a plague; they lit candles, started a Mexican wave of 24-7 prayer. The neo-scientologists dismissed this as nonsense, declaring that the jellyfish weren't jellyfish, and the stars weren't stars. Both were suspended strings of lights strung high above the horizon, but the fore-fathers had built them wrong. Instead of LEDs they'd chosen high-powered bulbs made from the same plastic commonly used for stress balls. When the cosmos compressed, the atmosphere clutched them too tightly. As these coloured bulbs popped, their innards fell as a gloop, like jellyfish sucked of all life.

For others, the answer was simpler. The night sky was an ocean. With the world upside down, gravity pulled the jellyfish Earth-wards. They died as they dived, bringing floods and chaos with them.

This wasn't the world's first or only type of falling: from apples and locusts to everyday weather. Even now, when a tiny dust particle high up in the Earth's atmosphere gets coated in water vapour, this freezes to create an ice crystal. As the crystal falls, it grows bigger, forming a perfect snowflake. Likewise, when nimbus-gathered water vapour turns to liquid, the falling raindrops are mostly welcomed by plants and open mouths. But this jellyfish slime wasn't a kind precipitation. It wasn't beautiful and it wasn't recyclable. Unlike normal rain, or even sleet, it did not rise up again to reform itself in clouds. Unbalanced, the world began to change; seas and land reformed themselves.

I've seen the old maps in the archives. News reports and statistics too. The Great Pacific garbage patch discovered in the 1980s was an early island of plastic, chemical sludge and rubbish that massed on our polluted oceans, trapping and killing marine wildlife. Later, folks like me used them as floating camps; some established archipelagos of flotislands.

I still remember the first one we found. We'd been living on a yacht that Ned patched up.

'Maybe this time…' He loosed the seagull from his hands like a raucous flapping wish.

We were close to giving up hope when the bird returned, an aluminium ring-pull in its beak.

'Like Noah!' Ned exclaimed.

The floating island of rubbish that the gull had found wasn't pretty and stank something awful until we got used to it. But we were used to getting used to lots of things by then, and it withstood the ocean waves better than our makeshift boat.

Two months later, we were still living there, foraging off the waste and making do. Though the squawking gulls swooped continuously overhead, not one had come back with a single leaf. I couldn't shake the sense of them swarming around us like landfill flies. We took to the yacht again.

This scragg of real land that we live on now used to be ten times bigger, with less swamp and free from nets of drifting plastic. Annual rainfall here increased by five per cent in just twenty years in the late twentieth century. Elsewhere, the North Pole lost 35% of its ice by 2016, with global temperatures 1.1° higher than in the pre-industrial era. That year, NASA climate scientist Gavin Schmidt spoke to Sarah Kramer at *Business Insider*. Her article warned, 'In our best-case scenarios, oceans are on track to rise 2 to 3 feet (0.6 to 0.9 metres) by 2100. Even a sea-level rise below 3 feet (0.9 metres) could displace up to 4 million people.'

But that prediction was then, before the last falling with its floods. They over-estimated with their forecast of only once a hundred years. When the jellyfish fell in 2035, the year before I was born, experts revised their guess to every forty or fifty. Myself, I'm sure the next downpour is coming sooner, a deluge of dead sky-swimmers like we've never seen: tentacles, umbrellas and slushy gloop no longer recognisable as aquatic flesh.

Watching the horizon now, listening to our current rain,

hearing the whisper of the last remaining star-gazers as they loose their leaves earlier, later, unsure of the seasons' change, the effect is always the same: my eyes water with pain, though I refuse to melt and cry. My tears would be a rising sea, not a snowflake gaining sparkle.

Ned and I have made our preparations. If the next fall comes before the planet's ready, we won't join the old men standing like weak Canutes, trying to push back the tides while surf licks at their knees, hips, waists; dead jellyfish pelting around them. We won't be caught taking trash out, carrying shopping or even mid-kissing. When it comes, we'll be on the highest ground left, knees planted firmly in the mud, pushing in new seeds.

Sources
Articles (alphabetically by title)

'Great Pacific garbage patch', Wikipedia <https://en.wikipedia.org/wiki/Great_Pacific_garbage_patch>.

'Melting of the North Pole', acciona <http://www.activesustainability.com/climate-change/melting-north-pole/>.

'25 Months Old, Rain O' Fish', 14 November 2017, Jellyfish Review <https://jellyfishreview.wordpress.com/2017/11/14/25-months-old-rain-of-fish/>.

Articles (alphabetically by author)

Kramer, Sarah, 'This Is What Earth Will Look Like in 100 Years', 17 August 2016, Business Insider <https://www.sciencealert.com/this-is-what-earth-will-look-like-in-100-years>.

Quilty-Harper, Conrad, 'Interactive graphic: UK rainfall in every year since 1910', 3 Jan 2013, The Telegraph <http://www.telegraph. co.uk/news/weather/9777749/Interactive-graphic-UK-rainfall-in-every-year-since-1910.html>.

Beachsidepotter
Susan E Barsby

The moonlight stretches long on the water, like a cheap water-colour, but the street-lights twinkling in the reflection are the only movement. The sea is calm now. The day's activity has been wiped away and only a few pieces of detritus have been left behind among the footprints in the sand.

Gina walks the same stretch morning and evening, up with the gulls and down with the gloom. In summer, mornings are easy. The winter shore is different and she often reverses her routine of walking before tea, to wait for the daylight. Each day she collects up what she finds. The council have cleaners but to be really effective requires constant patient work on a detailed scale. The day-trippers' rubbish is the most obvious: disposable nappies, plastic bottles, crisp packets all strewn ugly, gaudy, tucked half in shame between stones despite the bin standing only a few feet away.

Off-season finds are often more interesting: plastic of all kinds – Lego, drinking straws, deflated balloons, random coloured shapes; lengths of twine; sea glass dulled and smoothed by the salt water; wood from crates or from trees, some pieces bleached by the sea, others rotting from the water, more still carrying Goose Barnacles clinging to the timber. Not long ago she came across a large plank covered with strange blue iridescent eggs, safe inside their casing but an eerie glow emanating from within.

She started off by taking much of this home but the cottage began to resemble a junk-yard, filled with the confusion of a hoarder and so she has learned to dispose of the rubbish properly. The drier wood she saves for the stove, the Lego and plastic can all be recycled, the twine usually thrown in the bin. Only the sea glass remains on the shore.

The morning's finds are photographed and placed on Instagram and Tumblr, a record for her followers.

Sometimes, when the need takes her, she leaves her house during the day and goes back to the beach. She always regrets it. The intrusion of others means her affinity with the ocean has gone. The winter months are better for lunchtime visits, and there can be days when she sees no one but a few oyster-catchers. The local dog walkers are regular in their habits and can be avoided.

This morning dull grey skies are reflected in the water, making it seem dirty looking and full of dust. It is only on close inspection that she can see how clear the water actually is. She prefers blue mornings with an early sun but the winter sea is a companion still, despite its drab appearance. The town looks shabbier in the off-season, boarded up in places, and the bright lights on shop windows piled with last season's multi-coloured goods look tired and desperate. With the first burst of spring the shop-keepers appear with pots of paint, new displays and a winter's worth of ideas to try and winkle out a few more pounds from the tourists. Gina bypasses them all and sticks to her section of the coast path.

At first she thinks it's the drag lines of a boat pulled up the sand but looking closely she sees other marks. At regular intervals on each side of the drag, there is an oval shape full of clumps of sand, sucked up into little mounds. She kneels to examine them, little hillocks, fairy sandcastles. The drag marks glisten in the morning light almost as if something has been spilled there. It's opalescent, shimmering, and she considers returning to the cottage to call the council about a possible chemical accident. But looking again she sees it's different. She pokes the sand with a stick peering in at the shine. It's mucus, strung along the sand and in places it's mixed with what looks like blood.

She sits back on her heels and realises it's quieter than usual. There are no birds today. The only sound is the waves breaking, their rhythm steady but subdued. Her walk is interrupted by a call. She looks up to see Mr Hogan crossing the sand towards her.

'Have you seen Milly?' he asks. His terrier, regularly walked along here, an ankle nipper. 'I let her off the lead and she's disappeared. It's not like her to run off.'

She shakes her head.

'Sorry. I'll keep an eye out.' He carries on along the beach before she can ask about the trail, catching a bit of mucus on his foot. He shakes it off and it flies a short distance, clumping up and shrinking down in the sand as it lands, catching the light again. She turns her attention back to the trail and follows it further up the beach to the cave. There is more blood here and, she notices, paw prints. They lead into the cave but don't appear to have come out again. She turns to see where Mr Hogan is but he is beyond hearing her call. She takes a few steps towards the cave entrance, and catches the smell for the first time. The salty, bitter smell of seaweed but with a hint of something else, something rotting. There is a sound from within, a whisper or a breath, and then silence. She peers into the darkness but instinct tells her not to go further. At least not without a torch. And a companion.

Gina heads home and makes a cup of tea, cupping it with her hands in an effort to soak up as much heat as possible. Once finished she sets to work as usual, but finds it hard to concentrate and much of the day passes with her gazing out of the window. There are still no birds, nothing she can hear.

The clock dings three and she can no longer contain herself. Grabbing her torch, a thick waterproof coat and phone, she pulls on her boots and heads back outside. She was going to call for a neighbour to come with her but she sees a man already on the beach and decides he will do.

He looks up as she gets closer and from the way he looks at her she knows immediately that he's seen the cave, knows something about it. He's wearing a waterproof jacket with an official looking insignia on the front. She nearly turns back but he gestures to her.

'Are you 'Beachsidepotter' by any chance?' he asks. Her Instagram name. She nods.

'Who are you?'

'Jack Devereux, I'm with the coastguard, special marine branch,' he thrusts his hand out and shakes hers with vigour. 'I'm afraid I can't let you go in the cave.'

'Why? I mean, I wasn't, I mean, how did you…?'

'It was you that helped us find her,' he says. 'Your picture of the eggs a few weeks ago, we follow all the beachcombing accounts. That and the marks on the sand this morning. We track them you see, the adults, but her signal faded. An attack, we think. But here she is, she made it.'

'I don't understand.'

'You don't need to. We'll be by later with some more information if you like but for now I need you to return home please.'

She looks out to sea, frowning, and sees a boat some way out. It has the same insignia painted on the prow.

'I've never heard of the special marine branch,' she says, unwilling to yield easily to his demands, however polite. 'What's your remit?'

He regards her closely, a smile forming at the corners of his mouth. He is, she notices now, quite attractive in a rugged outdoorsy way and she can picture him in an advert at the back of the Sunday supplements.

'We track creatures,' he says. 'Portuguese Man-O-War, Giant Squid, that sort of thing.'

'Really. And then what?'

'Care and protect, that's our motto.'

'So the cave, that's what? A squid?'

'We'll classify it later. I need you to return home now. We'll close off the beach for a while.'

'For a squid? You already said you'd tracked it. You must know what it is.'

'Now Miss, if you please.' He has stopped smiling now and a voice comes from the radio clipped to his belt. She shakes her head and turns away.

Back home she switches her laptop on and Googles the special marine service. Their official government page is full of the same bland lines he's just told her, almost word for word. But she finds more information elsewhere. There are extensive forums and she gets sucked in to the comments. Some of the theories are fantastic but the fervent passion of the contributors is absorbing and an hour passes before she knows it.

There is a sound. A shout? And a rumbling. She jumps up and pulls her boots back on, runs outside. It is nearing darkness now and difficult to see but there is some kind of movement on the beach.

A slurping sucking sound and then a splash.

Silence.

She sits on the sand and waits, certain something will happen. She is unsure how long she waits. There is a voice.

'Is anyone there? Milly?'

'Mr Hogan, it's Gina. Down here.'

'Has it gone?'

'I'm not sure. I think so.'

'Did they take it?'

'I don't think so. I didn't see.'

He sits beside her.

'Have you seen the cave?'

'He wouldn't let me.'

'No, I mean since. Look.' She can feel rather see him point and turns to follow his finger.

A light, dim but constant, shines from the cave. It is the same blue glow that she found on the eggs last week and now it pulsates softly. It's hypnotic and the two of them stare at it for a long time.

'We should keep warm,' he says finally. It is clear they are going to stay on the beach until first light and she agrees. At her cottage she directs him to the cupboards where her blankets and groundsheet are stored while she makes up hot chocolate with brandy and finds a woolly hat.

They return and bundle themselves up. There is no sound. Even the sea seems to be holding its breath. Gina finds herself nodding off, something she didn't think would happen, and she jerks awake.

'It's all right,' said Mr Hogan. 'If you want to.'

When she comes to, he has gone. The flask lies on his discarded blanket but there is nothing else nearby except marks in the sand. She follows them down to the shore and floating on the water she can see the insignia from Jack Devereux's jacket.

The sun emerges from behind a cloud and lights up the beach. It's a picture of peace. Oyster catchers appear on the shore; herring gulls soar overhead.

Gina photographs the insignia, returns to her cottage and posts it on Instagram.

Seal Boy
Sarah Evans

Up here on a summer day, I can gaze out towards where the sky comes down to meet the curve of the sea and, choosing my direction, standing just so, I glimpse the thin line of blue land emerging from nowhere, barely there at all.

But the mists have settled on the tops now. The birds have gone, their ledges left to vetch and sea thrift, the air no longer filled with their squabbles; there's just the whistle of the wind and the crash of ocean rollers. Standing a few fearful feet from the edge, where the land plunges away, the breeze plays its games, whipping me round till it might almost take me stumbling over and down. The horizon is a grey blur and I have the feel there's nothing else out there, nothing at all, that we're the only people in existence.

It's then I see it. An unsettled glimpse. Something.

Immediately I wonder if I'm not mistaken, fooled by a mischief of the ocean, a misguidance of light.

But again. Something.

Just a trick of the eye. Some flotsam or a seal, yet I know it has to be more than that, else it's nothing at all.

A boat.

It isn't one of ours, not on such rough seas. I peer into the gloom, hoping for a second sighting, but all I see is the heave of waves, their smooth humped backs.

The light is touching Maein's crag on Oiseval as I hurry back, my feet finding their holds over the mist-slickened rocks. The basket full of peat is unwieldy against my hip, and I know I've gone up higher, taken longer, brought back less than I should have done.

The men are back from the Gathering, working the fields. Father rakes over our plot readying it for the barley, and I stop a few feet back from where his back is hunched against the effort and I wait for him to notice me.

He stops after a little while and looks up. 'Skena.' He nods and waits for me speak.

It sounds unlikely now I put this thing into words, and I see him thinking how maybe I was imagining. But he puts the hoe down and goes to talk to some of the other men and they pull on their sheepskin coats, and set off towards the Landing. I leave my basket behind and I follow.

Others are already gathered from the Village, all looking out the same way. The waves ride high away from the shore, the tops flattened by the wind that sends up sheets of spray, reaching us where we stand so we taste the salt. The ocean crashes, breaks and splutters onto the skerries guarding the entrance to the bay, causing whirls and eddies in the space between.

My father joins Èildear Graye, standing beside him on the flat stones a little to one side. He follows the line of Graye's arm as he points outward, and my own eyes follow too. There's a fleck of black against the turmoil of grey-green, there, then gone, the angle of the vessel all wrong as if it's about to dive down into the depths, like a fulmar, or a seal.

The rumours bubble and spread. *Two men have been sighted.*

We watch from the shore. Impatience presses, my fingers clenching tight with the desire for us to do something, to help, yet knowing that heading out would be a kind of madness and besides we have reason enough to be wary of strangers. There's nothing to be done, yet it feels wrong, this spectating, yet neither can we go on our way and about our business. The waves part. I see them for the first time, two lonely figures. They raise their hands towards us and I think I hear them hailing on the wind, not the sounds of the words, but their shape. Pleading. Hopeless. Or perhaps it's nothing but the cry of a lonesome wintering bird. The boat is so close to the stacs and there's no steering of it. It misses, but narrowly. It keels almost over. It rights itself, is lifted up and crashes back onto the rocks.

My fingers let go their grip. The silence is terrible as people stand and stare at the wreckage and then start to turn away, thinking back on the work they have abandoned.

'No, look!' The voice is high and urgent and it's a moment before I properly know that it's my own, just as it is my arm pointing out there to what I see.

Around me people shake their heads. But then there's another hand pointing and another. A seal-head is bobbing in the water. But it isn't a seal.

We stand under the same spell as before, unable to move, watching the slow battle, waiting for the moment the head dips from sight and does not emerge.

There's a flurry of movement now amongst the men; Èildear Graye is at its centre and he's shouting instructions, and though there's been no Gathering to give consent to this, the men go and get the rope which has been stored away for next year's fowling.

The younger men move as one, Barday at their front, wrapping the end tightly round his middle, as if for stepping over the cliffs; he walks down to the water's edge. I think of Toren, his younger brother, going over to the sickness last winter, and my own hopes dying too.

Barday walks into the incoming waves and another follows behind, and so on, all of them forming a line of rope and man, stretching out into the sea, the water crashing over and around, the other end held firmly by those on shore, Father among them. The seal-head is still there, bobbing into sight, out of it, and the rope is pulled as far as it will go but still with a gap, one they can't seem to close.

I screw my eyes tight, as if my own wanting can make a difference. When I look again, the men are retreating back, and at first I think it's over, they've abandoned their folly of a plan, but then I see how they are pulling on something, a dark, limp shape. They pull him onto the stones, his body slack, like a dead seal. I go closer, wanting to see, wanting not to, joining the circle of lookers-on, all of us just looking. Idle. Helpless. Èildear Graye is kneeling beside the body, pulling him up and forward and thumping him on the back.

The body shudders. We onlookers jump back, fearful of some unnatural thing, a spirit back from the dead. But he's just a half-drowned man.

He begins to splutter and cough something awful. Water seems to pour from him, as if it's filled him up, his belly and lungs, his very veins, and all of it is spilling out to rejoin the mother ocean.

He starts shivering, shaking so much you'd think his bones would be rattling, and that we'd hear it along with the chattering of teeth. Èildear Graye has his arms round the man's shoulders now, and I see how he's not much more than a boy, caught between one thing and another.

I step forward, a daring taking hold, slipping my thick shawl from my shoulders and spreading it across his. The wind blows chill through the wool of my dress. Crouched down beside him, this boy from the sea, my hand brushes his neck and he's cold like a fish and I see how his hair is light in colour as straw, his skin is pale and green. His head is down to his chest, but his fingers, blue, clutch the edge of the shawl. Èildear Graye moves to draw it tighter round, allowing me a nod and one of the men casts his coat atop.

I have no further reason to stay. I feel the heat rising in my cheeks and step back. I begin to walk away, fearful of being thought too bold, too foolish. I avoiding looking for Father's gaze, and, as I walk back, my arms wrapped tight around under my chest, I think of Mother and how cross she will be about my lack of prudence.

I reach our homestead just as the light is hitting the slopes of Mullack Bi, casting a soft orange glow over the green, signalling how the day is almost done, yet none of my chores finished. Back home, I linger in the doorway as I tell the tale, expecting a scolding, but Mother just makes her *tch-tch* sound and beckons me close to the fire. She goes out to storage and returns with a worn and moth-eaten replacement for my lost shawl, one that smells of damp and dead birds.

I'm ablaze with wanting to know more. I should work all the harder, making up for the lost hours, but my mind is everywhere but on what I should be doing.

The sun is almost gone, a bright smudge behind the hills, when I spot them along the path, a small group of men heading our way, and amongst them a cart. My eyes strain with wanting to see, but all I can make out is a dark bundle.

I'm fearful of what might emerge, a corpse, a dead thing, life having been surrendered.

Mother goes out a little way to greet the party. I see the brief words she and Father exchange, before Father and Graye lift the man, the seal-boy, one of his arms over each of their shoulders, carrying him the short distance to our dwelling. The boy is ghost pale and lacks the strength even to open his eyes, but there's a movement in his chest, a wheezing in and out of breath.

Mother bids me help. Bringing in straw and sacking to set up a crib in the kitchen. Building up the fire. Warming the ewes' milk we pulled this morning and bringing it to the boy, feeding it to him, spoonful by spoonful, his eyes only half open, looking nowhere, and most of the milk dribbling down his chin till he gets to retching again.

I set water to boil.

He's still wrapped in the shawl, fingers clutching the edges, and I have to ease them away one by one, his grip strong like a baby. The wool is caked in silt and sand, but not so much as his clothes, soaked through and clinging to his skin.

We start to undress him and, despite the way everything is heavy with dirt and salt, we see how the cloth is different, a tighter weave than from Father's loom. His pale skin is speckled with bruises which bloom green and yellow. His limbs are long and slender, his ankles so thin, twigs that might snap, and it's then I notice the strange forming to his toes which grow unnaturally straight, all in a line, like a row of close-seeded herbs. He shivers, mostly naked now, though his skin burns hot with fever. And my cheeks are burning too.

Once he is clean, we dress him in Father's clothes, and they are too wide, yet leave his ankles and shins sticking out of the bottom, along with those strange feet. He groans softly as if with a disturbed dream. Only once do his eyes open fully and stare into mine; his eyes are pale like the rest of him, blue like the sea on a clear day, rather than the colour of wood, of mud, of dried leaves. I murmur softly, the type of nonsense you might say to soothe a teething child and my hand brushes his forehead, running through the hair which is so very pale, with the flicker of the fire setting it ablaze. He settles then. Sleeps.

Nothing more is said as we occupy ourselves in the usual ways of cooking and eating. Of Mother and I spinning and Father at the loom. We remain at our work, light flickering from the lamp and the fire, before retiring to the side room and our beds, leaving the boy curled up before the dying embers. A curtain is drawn across the space, but I can hear the two of them, their low murmurings, the shuffle of bedclothes and the scratch of straw. And I feel alone, excluded from this closeness, from what passes between a man and woman in the dark.

Days and nights come and go to an unnatural rhythm, our routines and habits broken, everything suspended, as if for a seven-day of mourning when little work is expected to be done.

He does barely nothing but sleep. He wakes with fever and fear in his voice and his words make no sense. I stay with him, watching. I wait for Mother to call me away to attend to all the things that need doing, but she leaves me be. I cool his face with a wet cloth when the sweat runs. I lift milk and water to his lips and try to bring him to drink. I speak in a low murmur, telling him how he is safe now and will soon be well again. I claim him back from the sea.

At first people stay away, fearful of the stranger sickness that sometimes drifts in with shipwrecks. But slowly people come visit, bringing their curiosity along with gifts of driftwood, of eggs preserved in ash, dried puffin mear and the fulmar oil which I rub onto his chest and whose vile smell is said to clear away most ills. The stuffs we have little enough of since Father twisted his leg with the fowling and it never quite turned straight again. Mother keeps the visitors at the door; she leaves me to the tending of the boy and manages the cooking, the cleaning and the sheep and cows herself.

I keep on talking, or sometimes sing, and he seems to settle to the lull of my voice. Slowly he becomes more alert, his eyes wide with animal bewilderment. He eats more hungrily, mouth opening like a fledgling as I feed him porridge mixed with gannet eggs, until the day where his arm rises to take the spoon himself. There's a moment when his hand covers mine, and it sends a tingling through me, his sea-eyes looking into my own.

His strength returns, little by little. He sits, stands and walks one side of the kitchen to the other, his weight part resting on my shoulders. His skin has warmed from pale green to faintest pink. He begins to help, at first just Mother and me, and it is strange to see a man doing women's work, but he doesn't seem to mind it. Helping with the milking of the cow and ewes and the grinding of corn. With the gathering of peat and turf for burning. The carding and the spinning. Setting the puffin snares.

He is quiet the evenings we sit, the four of us, our eyes watching the dancing of the flames, fingers busy with our tasks. But by day, when it is just us two, working side by side, he talks, his way of speaking strange, and so many of his words unknown.

He does not understand all my words either and I have a sense of all the things I know, that I've learned from such an age so it seems I've always known them, our ways to doing things, now seeming curious through this seal-boy's eyes. Like when I take him to offer milk to the Milking Stone, so our cattle will produce a sturdy steam, or point out the pattern of the day by the light on the hills, or the ways we judge the coming fury of the wind and waves.

He tells of where he comes from and like the tales of faraway I've heard before, it is difficult to imagine they are true. He tells of lands where you can walk for days and still not come back to the place from whence you set out. His arm swings wide as if trying to properly describe such a thing. A land where you can walk so far from shore that people have never seen the sea, never tasted fish, nor heard the cry of gulls. He talks of villages so many times bigger than our own, places he calls towns and cities, where there are enough dwellings to cover the whole of our isle, leaving no room for the cattle and sheep and birds and rocks. Of market places selling all manner of exotic things, unknown foods, and cloths in many colours. Of something called *glass* that is hard and smooth which keeps the wind out but still allows you to see through, as if it was made of ice, and which, like ice, can offer your own reflection back. Of plants that he calls *trees,* which grow as tall as Maein's crag and so many birds and beasts we've never even known existed. Of *books*, where everything is marked down, like notching into a branch, yet somehow different, and managing to capture words themselves. And I wonder why he would ever have thought to leave such a place.

He smiles then, and looks down and talks about his *spirit of adventure.* He tries to tell me of that day, using his hands where the words fail us, of setting out in pursuit of a shoal of fish, so many of them, so quick and silver, and catching enough to fill the boat. Before the wind turned. The seas tossed the boat away from its path, leaving him and his companions adrift for several days and not knowing where they were or if they would ever see land again. He falls into quietness then, with a kind of sadness and I think that too much talking is not good, that understanding does not need so many words.

I take him up onto the cliffs. The birds have begun their return and they circle peaceably above, seeking materials for their nests. The grey mist remains and there is nothing to see of the blue land. Legs stretched out we see the difference in our feet and then he laughs and though I don't fully know why, I join him in his delight.

The next morning, Father beckons him to join the men for the daily Gathering. We see them later, the men heading for the hills, bringing down the sheep who are heavy with lamb. While they are gone, Mother bids me take the crib apart, the straw and sacking moved to the byre, alongside our cow.

I miss him by my side as I go about the tasks which now seem dull without the bright flash of his smile, and of his hair in the sun. But I am glad for his returning to strength.

One night I go to him, the byre filled with the loamy scent of animal and straw, together with the sharpness of burning oil. Sliding in beside him, the straw rustles beneath our weight. He smells of the sea. And, as our mouths join in hunger, I feel smooth and slippery beneath his hands, becoming seal-like too.

The moon dwindles bit by bit, before swelling whole again. Once then twice and my body does not follow in its rhythm. I wake to find bile rising hotly from my belly. Mother looks at me, she pulls me towards her, her hand resting on the swelling under my ribs.

She says nothing. But after a day or two, Father digs a pit just a few yards from the dwelling, lining it with peat and charcoal. A sheep is killed, the blood drained, the skin removed and we wake to the sweet scent of roasting meat. I smile at him, my seal-boy, this morning of our Joining and he looks at me, his look puzzled, and for a moment understanding between us seems to fall away.

He keeps that bewildered smile as the villagers start to gather to take us down to the Landing.

It's only then, standing there beneath the Mistress Stone, seeing how it curves so steep and high up to the jut of its chin, that my heart thinks to beat hard and fast, knowing what should come next, how a boy must prove himself, climbing to the very top and crouching low, balancing there on a single foot, declaring his ableness to keep a family.

Around me I glimpse the boys I grew up alongside, remembering back, the ways they would show off, long before they were of an age for their boldness to be real. The rock has never looked so treacherous, so lacking in forgiveness. I dare not glimpse my seal-boy's toes, and look instead at Father, hoping he will read the pleading in my eyes.

Father glances between the two of us. He casts an eye at Èildear Graye and perhaps there's a nod between them. Father beckons Laira forward, chosen as being the youngest of our near kin.

I know there will be some who say this isn't right. That my seal-boy should take his chance like any other and for a moment a cloud seems to dim the sun, even though the sky is clear.

Laira's face is oddly serious as she steps forward with a rope of twined flowers and leaves and gives it to my father. I take the seal-boy's hand and Father binds our hands together with the rope, a light bond, one that easily breaks to signify our joining in a stronger one.

He smiles more widely then, my seal-boy, as if finally grasping what this is about. His fingers interleave with mine and he pulls me close, his lips pressed first to my forehead and then my mouth. I turn my head, laughing to hide my blush. Others join their laughter to mine, but there is goodwill in it, accepting the strangeness to his ways.

Back at our dwelling, we eat and drink the nettle ale and eat the sweetly roasted lamb. The Èildears mark out time with sticks and whistles as we dance and sing and for today no one thinks of work, of lost boats, of the sickness that can come from nowhere, or of the cliffs.

The season turns; each day the light stretches a little longer, and there's a new warmth to the air. The mist that has shrouded us all winter begins to clear and I take him up onto the cliff tops and point out into the distance, the band of blue. His fingers hold mine tight, and his look is of a lost child. I take his hand and press it to where the baby swells, so he can feel how strongly it moves, this new life that grows more and more insistent. I take him to the edge, both of us cautious, and I show him the narrow ledges where the birds have built their nests, the eggs now hatched, the youngsters starting to grow. And my usual joy at the coming harvest, the days of plenty, is mixed, like mixing sweet berries with bitter herbs, feeling a fear and knowing he does not yet understand.

He has been here for seven swellings of the moon when it is time for the fowling. Father and he go to the Gathering, but we women have seen how the day is fair and other work already done in readiness. Mother and I, we meet with the other women and wait beneath the cliffs for what is to come.

He arrives alongside the men, walking just a little apart, without a look my way.

The birds glide effortlessly on the breeze, looking so peaceable up on high, but they won't yield their young, not without an attack of beak and claw and the spitting of the foul-smelling oil.

The cliffs have never seemed so high, the birds so much a menace, and I think back to the day of our Joining and I'm hoping Father will speak out, or someone will, to say how my seal-boy is not yet properly healed, that he's not had the practice in this, that where he comes from the boys do not spend their boyhood in climbing, learning to clamber up walls of stone almost before they can walk. He looks too tall, too slight, like a bush outgrowing itself, becoming thin and straggly and too much at the mercy of the wind.

I want to step forward and speak on his behalf, but it isn't my place to do so. No one speaks. He remains silent too.

I wait amongst the other women along with the older and less able men, at the ready to do those women's tasks, the careful collecting of the fulmar oil from the birds' gut, the slitting of the bodies from neck to tail and rubbing in of salt. The plucking of feathers. All the more minor tasks to our enterprise.

The men have removed their gannet-neck shoes and you can see the way our feet are different, our toes like birds' talons, able to curl and grasp.

Barday is among the first to go, climbing deftly, a four-footed animal, the rope coiled lightly around his shoulders and him snagging it against the rocks here and there to help those who follow. My seal-boy stands a little back, just watching, his skin yet more pale, his toes burrowing into the small stones as if shy to show their strangeness. I can see the tension in the long line of him, like a fishing line pulled taut by a fish, the struggle between two things, the wanting to be part of this and the fear. Others follow Barday, and my seal-boy watches, watches. But no amount of watching is the same as actually placing a hand into a hold and then a foot, and limb by limb hauling yourself upwards towards the sky and trying not to think of the drop below.

He steps forward.

I feel the fear flowing hot and cold inside my gut, as if it is me who is asked to do the climbing. I feel how the solid certainty of the ground gives way to the flimsiness of finger and toe-holds, how that seems such a fragile grasp on things. How the wind is trying to prise those slender digits free, and that's before you're up with the birds who defend their eggs with a ferocity it is hard to believe when you see them gliding so peaceably high above.

I squeeze my eyes against the sun, then squeeze them tighter, shutting them against bearing witness and then opening them. Unable to watch, unable not to. My palm rests on the swell where the baby grows, my breath trapped in my chest, my fingers tight with fear and hope, like the day he came to us from the sea.

The moon swells and ebbs and the seasons pass. I no longer find the time nor have the wish to look out to the horizon, as if I have found what I'm looking for. My gaze is lower now, the baby just beginning to find her feet, her neat rows of toes treading lightly over the yard, the treachery of the ground tripping her sometimes, but it isn't far to fall and it's a small part of what she needs to learn.

Last night, he dreamt of the sea, my seal-boy, a restlessness coming over him, and him drowning in sweat. I listened to his voice crying out. And though I gripped him tight, reeling him back in, I had that sense of losing him, of him never fully being mine.

He froze such a short way up, his seal-feet unable to grip.

People are kind enough and he does the work of women and older men, leaving the climbing to others. The fowls are our way of living, the meat and eggs, the oil and feathers, and though the harvest is shared, the larger part goes to those who pit their skill and lives against the cliff, the winds and the birds.

Amongst the men he stands apart; he minds it more than I do.

And on the mornings like today, after those nights of dreaming, when there's a chance it might be clear, I see him heading higher than needs be, climbing up onto the cliffs, and I know he will be looking out, gazing towards the thin blue line in the distance, thinking on all that he has left behind, the blue land he no longer speaks of.

The Sea Inside
Linda Maclennan

1.

The open-air swimming pool was a blue rectangle that shimmered from my window. To the right of the pool a large red crane loomed robotic over the rooftops. They were constructing more high-rise blocks of flats, a stark contrast to the red brick mansion that stood to the left of the pool. The extensive Victorian building, converted into flats, had seagull chicks nesting between the chimneys, their speckled heads visible against the moss-covered brick.

I remember when Stephanie moved into the top floor of the mansion a year ago. I wasn't a prudish old lady, but I noticed she walked about naked at night with her curtains open. Occasionally I saw her in the communal pool, her fair hair taking on a dark hue in the water. She wore a red swimming costume with floppy bows on each breast. I viewed her through a telescope, never growing tired of watching her swimming through the glittering blue water.

One day I noticed Stephanie talking to a man on the sunlounger next to hers. They had matching white towels. Later that evening they appeared in the window of her flat. The man pulled the curtains shut. Two months later they were still closed. A red light sifted through them at night. Stephanie no longer visited the pool or paraded naked about her room.

Six months later sirens filled the air - fire engines and ambulances screeched to a halt on the street below. A crowd stared up at the roof of the red brick mansion as ladders were raised from the fire trucks and firemen climbed onto the roof. There was no sign of smoke. The firemen had axes. They shouted down to everyone on the ground. 'Move away from the building!'

They hung safety nets from the guttering, harnessed themselves to the chimneys, and used their axes to smash the roof tiles. The red crane growled into motion, swinging its hook across the rooftops, lowering it through a gaping hole in the roof. I remember seeing a pink cloud floating overhead like a squashed-up face, features being pulled out of shape: a tight frown drifting into surprised agitation – pursed mouth flaring into a long-lipped smile. The cloud-face broke in half becoming two wispy mice.

The crane shuddered as the hook rose, the mechanics trembling. What could be coming through the roof?

It was a large blue-skinned creature on a stretcher. It reminded me of a blue whale. A bulging arm suddenly flopped from beneath a white sheet causing the whole structure to rock. The crane groaned as I watched the blue whale fly gracefully through the air. And even though I saw five fingers on the end of its flipper and hair resembling freshly cut corn I didn't make the connection. The body swam through the blueness of the sky, white sheet flapping. Through my telescope I saw a grey-blue mottled face with tightly puckered mouth. The shadow of the blue whale slid over the crowd below. The rectangle of swimming pool became the sea. I longed to see the huge mammal released, imagining it falling through the air in a swirl of blubber - a giant belly flop into the water: a splash that would cover the City with water awash with chlorine.

2

I've always liked roof gardens. A scrap of Eden suspended in the sky. My daughter, Donna, arrives with my food. We look out of the window together, side-by-side. She talks a lot, mumbling about the stairs and the broken lift.

'It's a good job you don't go out, Mum. It'd be a real expedition for you.'

I want to tell her that I travel in my head, down the stairs and along the pavement, even though my legs are withered. I try to speak, dribbling instead, and she wipes my mouth with a tissue. My curry is spoon fed, chicken floating in spiced butter. I chew and swallow, opening my mouth for more.

Oh yes, I tell her, although she can't hear me: I know who lives in the red brick mansion. I've seen their nameplates above little metal doorbells. Ding-dong. Mr Adams, the new tenant, with his lovely wife and daughter. The stick-thin daughter's name is Abigail. At the window she does the same thing as cats when they paw the glass in a frenzy trying to get in. Abigail is trying to get out. The roof garden has tomatoes in grow bags. She sits staring at them. Once she tried to climb out of the small top window. She was half way out, arms dangling, but her mother caught her just in time, yanking her back. She could have fallen I suppose. It's a long way down. I'd have climbed out of my own window, jumped across the rooftops and picked her half a dozen plump tomatoes if I could. She could have feasted on them and saved some for later.

I chew my curry. 'Bit gloomy out there today, Mum,' Donna says. 'Do you want some more of that sunflower seed bread? It's gone up again. The carer will come and put you to bed at 7. I'll call round tomorrow and bring you everything you need.'

I can't lift my arms so a telescope on a stand comes in handy as I love to watch people, but I'm not a stargazer or a peeping Tom.

If I nudge it with my chin to point to the far left I can see the wide blue sea. To the far right is a large rubbish dump where seagulls swoop down into the compound. Sometimes they fly back with bread in their beaks as their babies squawk, 'Feed me. Feed me,' from between the chimney tops. The dump has a mountain of rotting food large enough to feed a blue whale. I swallow the last mouthful of curry. Donna wipes my chin, telling me that all along Herbert Street there were objects dropped on the road: 'A mermaid ragdoll, a gardening glove, a straw hat, and then a tape measure.'

Assuming that someone might have dropped them by accident I assemble the objects in my mind – are they treasured belongings or discarded rubbish bounced out of an open-topped rubbish truck? I hear the door close. Donna has gone.

3.

Stephanie buys boxes of Belgium chocolates with pretty pink bows on the lid. She has a penchant for bows, attaching them to all her clothes. An elaborate satin bow decorates each of the posts of her four-poster bed, like four exotic butterflies about to take flight. Her red swimming costume is drying on the radiator. The bows are too floppy but she can't bear to part with it. She loves to swim in the local pool. The short walk takes her past the corner shop, which always has lovely displays of chocolates in the window.

Stephanie likes to do length after length, imagining she's swimming in the Bahamas. It's not hard to conjure up a palm tree or two. She can switch off the noise of police sirens, food delivery trucks, fire engines, and the growling throb of the red crane moving scaffolding about the sky.

In her bed she lets the chocolates melt on her tongue. They nourish her. When the sticky sweetness has slipped down her throat she places another one on her tongue.

At the poolside a man sits on the lounger next to hers; they have matching white towels.

'Would you like to come out for a meal?' he asks.

She blinks and shifts round to have a closer look. Very smooth skin, muscular, tattoos of snakes and ladders on one arm: Vince written in blue ink across his knuckles.

'Or if you like,' he adds, 'I could cook us a romantic dinner back at your pad…'

'It's a date,' she says, twirling the bows on her swimming costume like striptease tassels.

'Great,' he says. 'I adore a woman who likes her food.'

4.

In a former life the men who labored at the Bunavoneader whaling station had whale blubber on their hands. Trees blown out of shape by the wind, enclosed the old seaside church, and as Mary sang hymns in Gaelic she tasted salt on her lips.

Murdo held the hymn book with hands that had caressed Mary's skin, hands softened by whale oil, hands that had fired harpoon guns.

The harpoon gun was made of polished wood and attached to the deck; this held the steel harpoon and could be swivelled to line up with the body of a blue whale. The sharp point of the spear would split a large hole in the whale's smooth skin. Blood and surf foamed together, waves lapped in red washes against the boat. The bleeding body was puffed up with air to make it buoyant and towed back to Bunavoneader where it was hauled up the slipway and cut with knives. The men believed that if a whale evaded capture, the creature would roam the seas for centuries to come.

Mary now knew that whales did live for a hundred years, or more, and a recent report suggested two hundred years. She was hooked on nature programs and had always had a soft spot for David Attenborough. She remembered a short film featuring a magnificent blue whale, thirty metres long and weighing two hundred tons. David's voice was soothing; it calmed her:

'The mother's milk flows directly into the calf's mouth and the milk of marine mammals contains as much as 50 percent fat… The calf puts on the equivalent weight of an adult man in just one day.'

Mary thought about how they lived for all those days swimming in the wide blue ocean. No wonder they grew so big. Whales are born tail first so that they can use it to swim straight to the surface as soon as the head disengages. She could imagine the tiny whale calf swimming rapidly to take its first breath.

It was how the men earned a living, so their families could eat. In the remote Hebrides jobs were scarce. You killed whales or you starved. Their biggest catch was an eighty-five foot long blue whale, which produced 137 barrels of whale oil and 100 barrels of guano. It made good money back then.

When she was pregnant with Donna, Murdo would come home with tales of how they'd fared on *The Bowglass*. She remembered one time especially.

'We caught a big one today, Mary,' he'd said. 'By killing the calf we could disable the mother.'

It sounded horrible, but necessary, or they wouldn't have got her. Murdo said that the mother whale was willing to be butchered on the spot, rather than abandon her calf. They struck the baby. It only took one blow. The mother thrashed about in the water and wouldn't leave. It was as though an enormous harpoon held her, yet nothing prevented her from fleeing. The men knew it. It was one of their tricks. They had her right where they wanted her. Two blows. Three blows. Ten blows. She died fighting.

'No more,' she'd cried, hurrying away from him, feeling their child swimming buoyant in her womb. Back then she wondered if she'd have that same strength of maternal love to die for her child.

Murdo put food on the table, but as he dozed on his chair, food digesting in his stomach, Mary thought about the whale calf. The men never made the connection between their own children and the whale calves they killed. If she had done Murdo's job, if women had gone out on the boats, would they have been strong enough to allow these barbaric acts to occur? If their own babies had been starving back at home they'd have done it, wouldn't they? They wouldn't have had time for compassion.

It feels like a miracle for some people to see a blue whale in its natural habitat. Some have made it their life long ambition. It becomes an obsession. Good sightings are rare and no one has ever witnessed the birth of a blue whale calf. They give birth in private: far away in the deep, deep sea, elusive beasts that live to be pensioners.

The whaling station is old now. Closed down and redundant. They went back to see. It was eerie, a place steeped in melancholy. Towers of death, painted with words: sludge, whale oil, blubber, rusted saws with grizzled teeth; the ghosts of the gentle giants floating serenely through the deserted station. A horrible morbid beauty resided there.

The blueness of the water is numbing my senses; a stream of sporadic bubbles leaves my mouth: white pearls of air. I swim on my back below a blue whale. The body is a like a bruised cloud above me. My stomach is throbbing and I can feel a flutter, the tiniest legs kicking through a cerulean sea, two arms like cotton threads undulating in the fluid of my womb. The haunting sound of the whale's song comes in waves, mixing with the water swirling around my ears.

The whale sinks. Its underbelly slides over my skin. The movement is gentle. On and on we swim, our stomachs touching. We are giving birth. As the blue whale moves away there is a feeling of release and I see the calf make an agitated movement with its tail. I push, feeling the head of my baby between my legs. A spin of bubbles as the calf breaks the surface. I hear a baby crying as we're hauled up from the deep.

'Mary. It's here,' Murdo says flatly. He looks over at the nurse holding our baby.

'You have a daughter,' she says.

'Pass her to me, Murdo…'

His hands fumble as our daughter screams. I embrace her, thinking of the blue whale calf swimming off with its mother.

My husband touches my shoulder and I recoil because he has whale blood on his hands.

5.

'Mum, the red brick mansion is sealed off,' Donna says peering out the window. 'There are police cars, ambulances, and several TV reporters. I don't know what's going on.'

I mean to ask if she still likes tomatoes, but I dribble instead. As a child she ate them like apples. I remember her on the tartan picnic rug, tomato pips wedged in the gap between her two front teeth. Later, when she was older, her friend told her they were fruit. And I couldn't help telling her the same old joke: 'Now I'll be serving your tomatoes with custard.' Did she ever laugh as gleefully as me?

She does her usual rounds of the small flat, scoops empty toilet roll tubes into my recycling bag, puts lids back on the jam and tea caddy, plumps up my pillows, turns the pages of the diary she bought me for my birthday. They are empty. I never write anything. My hands are too arthritic to hold a pen. All my thoughts are carefully stored inside my head.

Donna picks up a tissue from the table and wipes my mouth.

Do you still like tomatoes? They used to be your very favourite. You used to sit on the rug and I'd cut cherry tomatoes into quarters. You used to suck out the pips.

She feeds me lasagne from a tinfoil tray. She doesn't bother with dinner plates: it creates more washing up. She holds up a glass of lemonade so I can suck it through a straw. Suddenly she becomes animated: 'Did I tell you about this doctor at work?' Donna works as a receptionist at Manor Road Surgery. 'She's as big as a house, yet she was in the staff room talking about the fat pills she was on. She was informing another colleague that she could still enjoy her cheats because the pills did all the work. She basically said she could have her cake and eat it, that the pills made the fat pass straight through. I couldn't believe I was listening to a senior doctor talking about fat pills.'

I think about the whale calf, how very rare it is for whales to give birth to twins because the mother can only nourish one baby. It sets me thinking of Murdo again, lurking in the shadows. I can almost hear him whisper: *Now your breast falls free on the face of another. The small mouth sucking. You nourish her.*

I started to despise my husband, not wanting him touching me like before. I spent time with Donna, besotted, as though

I was an addict, watching her for hours. I closed my ears to Murdo's tales of death. My relationship with my husband changed. I was done with sexual intimacy. Initially there were three of us, but Murdo became an outsider: soon it was just the two of us.

6.

Vince stresses that I don't have to lift a finger. There's a never-ending supply of chocolate in pink boxes tied up with silver ribbon. My four-poster bed has become a palace: gold netting and red velvet cushions to support my growing body.

It excites Vince when I stand on the special scales he's bought: four foot square in heavy-duty steel. He's been researching ceiling hoists then I won't have to get up at all. When I put on weight, especially when it's over five pounds, Vince says it's celebration time. My goal is to reach 41 stone. Some feedies die in their sleep because their vital organs are crushed by the excess weight.

Vince says I'm beautiful as he jiggles my stomach with soft, smooth hands. He sets up all my equipment: funnels, tubes, costumes with feathers, sequins, and bows; brushing my hair into sleek coils and whispering that I'm his voluptuous mermaid. He puts a tiara on my head, glitter on my eyelids, and an aqua shawl draped over my body. Sometimes after alcohol the shawl slips off whilst Vince's camera is running. We're doing a video blog. I tell the camera that I've put on extra weight and we crack open the Champagne.

In my dreams I'm running, although in reality I can hardly walk.

Vince gives me bed baths, cleaning between the folds of my flesh, rubbing my body with Baby Oil. He measures my thighs daily, recording it in the 'Fat is Beautiful' notebook. Vince makes me six large meals a day. Breakfast is twelve fried eggs, ten slices of toast with lashings of butter, six sausages, two pounds of bacon, and a whole black pudding. If I get indigestion Vince hands me a glass of milk of magnesia and I carry on. In between meals I have some of my 'feed'. He mixes it up in a special container, attaching it to the top of the four-poster bed, so that the tube hangs down like a giant straw. I can suck the buttery feed into my mouth as I relax.

If I tell Vince I'm fit to burst he gets a panic in his eyes. 'We're not going to meet our target, honey. What are we going to celebrate if you don't gain this week? Come on and eat another spoonful for Vince. My beautiful soft baby girl.' If I vomit he has to use the funnel, pouring the rich nourishment down my throat, and he's right, the look of pleasure on his face when I've gained another ten pounds is worth all the effort.

7.

Abigail's happy face is on the TV screen. Girl found starved to death in Brighton. I stop chewing my lasagne, tomato sauce gagging in my throat. All I can see are the plump tomatoes that were growing on the family's roof garden.

'Not hungry?' Donna says. 'Come on, you don't want to waste it; there's nothing of you. I'll put it in the fridge. The carer can warm it up later in the microwave.'

8.

It is possible for a whale to starve.

Their main food is krill; a single blue whale can eat 40 million krill a day. David Attenborough says if toxic chemical sludge continues to be pumped into the sea the krill will die. It's the everyday litter that finds its way into the ocean: plastic bags performing mad swirling dances in the wind, whisking around in the air before diving into the sea. The waves carry the water-sodden bags down to the bottom of the ocean where crabs scuttle sideways across the white polythene. The carriers that hold my groceries. The bags that carry my fish and chips from the local *Frydays* chip shop. Whales choke as the plastic fills their stomachs: a rubbish dump in the belly of a whale and no seagulls to fight for the pickings.

9.

Mr Jonathan Adams likes to peer into private places. When his thin wife, Sue, is asleep on the sofa, he uses his credit card to access the dark net where Halosdyne, 'of the sea', resides in a room lit by a red light bulb. His eyes flicker, pausing on the hot pulsating body that lies on a four-poster bed. He licks his lips as the flesh rolls with a blur of green feathers, sequins and sparkling blue latex. The camera zooms in on Halosdyne's mouth glistening with red lipstick and particles of double cream from the éclair she's just eaten.

'35 stone and counting…' she says as her mouth stretches into a smile. She opens her lips to accommodate another chocolate éclair, white cream smearing on her chin: she licks it off with a long pink tongue.

Somewhere in the flat Jonathan has a daughter.

He puts headphones on, turning the volume up. Throbbing music plays as Halosdyne starts her striptease; her movements are deliberately slow, each second tots up another pound.

Triple cheeseburger with extra cheese and bacon slices; three portions of French fries; two litres of Pepsi cola; a family sized trifle with double whipped cream; two packs of ham, shaped and formed from bits of pig: eyes of pig, nose of pig, ear of pig, tail of pig, and fat of pig, so tasty on the tongue, swallowed down with two more litres of fizzy cola; jam roly-poly and custard; spotted dick; bread and butter pudding; buttery feed through a tube.

Abigail can see the ocean, but she can't touch it. On her bedside cabinet there's a picture book of a mermaid who lives under the sea. Marina and the Silver Shell. Marina has a green, shimmering tail and lives in an underwater castle. She rides on the backs of whales, even though they're big and she's small.

Abigail is hungry. The tomatoes glow red on the roof outside.

10.

Blue whales don't eat man. He wouldn't be able to slip through the baleen, the whale's spaghetti-like teeth that hang down like a curtain.

It's the sperm whale that can gobble up a man: the biggest animal to devour with its teeth. They feed on squid, octopus and large fish, but once in a while a man will fall into the water from the deck of a boat. In the deepest oceans off the north west coast of the Outer Hebrides, if the sea is rough enough, the boat will tip sideways. A man will slip and slide off the deck and a sperm whale will get to swim away with the man in his stomach.

Murdo was swallowed by a whale. *The Bowglass* took a battering from the creature at first, a harpoon skimmed the female's back and it nudged the boat, rocking it violently. It was then that Murdo lost his footing. As I listened to the news I held Donna in my arms, unable to cry.

11.

Nature has a way of balancing out food. A whale might wake up one morning and not have enough to eat, surviving on water alone; a natural fasting period ensues causing it to lose a layer of fat or two. It might hit an area where man's insatiable appetite for carbon has warmed the ocean and depleted the krill; the Earth-encircling blanket of greenhouse gases too cosy for the two-inch shrimp.

But a week later the whale might come upon a feast, hungry belly growling, the equivalent of an all-you-can-eat buffet. Krill would be abundant; the whale would gorge, filling itself up to ensure it didn't starve the next time it ran into a famine. That's the way things are in nature. Whales don't overeat. David Attenborough says so. And when a whale dies naturally, it sinks down to the bottom of the sea to provide a feast for all the other creatures that crawl or swim in the depth of the ocean. It's an ecosystem. If you mess with that you create an imbalance that will wipe out the world.

12.

Marina and The Silver Shell
The coral tables were filled with jellyfish trifle, seaweed stew, and blue lagoon ice cream. Marina blew on her silver shell and all the fish in the sea came through the doors to her palace. They ate till dawn and danced in the ballroom all the next day and into the night. The music flowed through the sea, and the whales sang, and the sailors in their ships looked down into the water and smiled.

13.

The push bike ridden by old Kenneth Macleod was gaining speed; his ride back from the tavern was downhill through the park.

When the push bike rode into Mary and Donna on their picnic rug, Mr Macleod was quick to slur his apologies. Mary rubbed her head and told him not to worry. It was only a small bang: an unfortunate accident. She'd wiped the tomato pips from Donna's mouth, folded the tartan blanket up, and wheeled the pushchair home. It might have been the handle bar, pedal, or edge of Kenneth's boot that made impact. Five-year-old Donna said she remembered silver wheels spinning, the tartan rug being gathered in a heap, her mother's arms springing out to protect her.

A week later Mary cooked herrings on the old black range and Donna heard a clatter of pans. Her mother had collapsed in a heap, spatula still in hand. Donna managed to alert Mrs Maclean, their neighbour, who was smoking in her garden and saw Donna's little face through a hole in the fence.

Mary recovered yet she wasn't the same, something to do with her brain exploding in on itself: tiny pops, sparks, red dots, black floaters, and prickles of pain. She had a numbness to her legs, a deadening of her thoughts. Who was this smiling child with a spoon in her hand? Was it really her daughter? She would sometimes take an hour or two to remember a name. 'It's Donna.' 'My husband is called Murdo.' Her brain would then rush and pulsate with colour, sound, and remembered memories: faces, places, voices.

The false memories began right there and became a part of everything.

14.

Donna drives through town. *The Bengal Star* is open for curry as usual, yet today she doesn't stop. A white carrier bag blows up off the road and whisks across the windscreen; the litter problem is getting worse. Bins spill over onto the pavements. Up in a Victorian tower block a window that once twinkled with the shiny lens of a telescope stands out because of its emptiness.

Her mother had loved whales. She had loved Donna with a passion, too, despite the strokes that made her grow weaker. Donna knew that Mary had leapt to protect her on that fateful day, preventing the wheel of Kenneth Macleod's bicycle from mowing her down. Her mother had taken the full impact.

The last stroke, two years back, had been the worst. It had taken her speech forever. She'd stopped asking if Donna wanted custard with her tomatoes. It had all gone.

Donna throws the broken plates and discoloured Tupperware into black sacks. There are letters tucked away. Diaries too. It's funny hearing her mother's voice after years of silence.

Of course her father, Murdo, wasn't in the belly of a whale. Mary had made that up, a false memory; Murdo being swallowed by a whale seeking revenge became a convenient fantasy. The ghost of that whale had swum through the old whale station at Bunavoneader, large and silent, void of song.

In a bid to escape Murdo, and her life in the Hebrides, Mary had written to her Aunt Dolina in Brighton. Her aunt understood her situation fully, having once eloped with an English man to escape the grey mists, rain, and bleakness of Harris. Mary packed some of their belongings and they fled to Brighton, sleeping on the train, waking to a bright new place: the other side of the world, or so it seemed. It was the safe side of the sea, uninhabited by whales, where men didn't harpoon mammals and talk of killing techniques.

Relatives put it down to the bang on the head, saying she didn't know her own mind. Yet Aunt Dolina was there to make sure she wasn't dragged back.

And the stories Mary told Donna were straight out of a fairy tale. 'Your daddy was swallowed by a whale. Very *Moby Dick*. The whales got their revenge on your daddy. He was killing their babies. If somebody tried to kill you, I'd...'

But *The Bowglass* had been real and Murdo's tears genuine when he'd come across the land to find them.

'It's too late,' she said, not blinking when tears ran down her husband's cheeks.

'Mary, have you no heart at all?'

Mary felt like screaming at him, about whales and blood and babies because she was sure that Murdo was the one without a heart.

He went back to Harris and left them far behind.

At the dump the seagulls fly away with week old curry pieces. The sunlight is blinding white, as the shrieking of the birds brings her to reality. She cries, watching all the paper tissues that have wiped her mother's mouth turn somersaults in the air.

On the rubbish dump Donna sees people's possessions piled up: a sequined mask with gold shells around each eye, a book called: *Marina and The Silver Shell,* a plastic funnel, tinfoil trays, whale posters, the ripped polythene of a grow bag, a tartan rug, a handful of red bows, a bent up bicycle wheel, and a telescope.

Over to the left of the dump she sees rats gathering in grey clusters. They watch her with hungry eyes. She picks up the telescope. It was her mother's eyes. She can't leave it for the rats to scurry over.

15.

The sea inside Mary is overflowing. As the real world shrinks, the ocean expands in her mind. The sea laps on the shores of Brighton, the open-air swimming pool spills over, and there are news reports of flooding all over the country.

The sea rises slowly and covers the land from the far reaches of Scotland to the underbelly of the Isle of Wight. It submerges the Hebrides, the Inner and the Outer, and whales swim over the land, swallowing people and trees and cars and houses made of brick and bridges made of stone. As they swim they sing, because all human noise has gone. The ships' throbbing engines are silent allowing males to call to the females, sending their haunting crics through the water so they will never become lost again. Never starve. Never die.

Mary wants to say that a 60 foot sperm whale carrying the body of Murdo is doing a bloated ballet over the Houses of Parliament, and that the trapped bodies of politicians spring like seaweed from the ornate windows, moving in the undulating rush of the water, arms rising in graceful arcs, long and short tresses dipping and darting, sparkling with tiny trapped bubbles, Champagne lightness in their hair.

The Men of the Nets
Lydia McGill

My dreams are blue and I wake up shivering. It's early. Lucretia didn't shut the window properly and my face is wet. I dab my eyelids with cold fingertips. The quilt is on the floor. I assume I must have kicked it there again, and step over it on my way to the bathroom.

The sea is placid this morning, merely a kindly mumble as it awakens, yawns, and stretches across the sand. It pacifies me with shushing as I splash my face, like a mother soothing her yowling infant. Leaning on the sill above the sink, I peer through the salt-flecked window down to the beach. The shore is empty and the fishermen are nowhere to be seen, not yet a single disturbance in the waves to herald trawlers chugging back towards land. Eventually I yield to the water's lullabies, slip on my espadrilles and blue dress, and leave the cottage.

The walk downhill makes my calves tighter than ever, and I bend my knees excessively with each step so as to stretch them out behind, flexing the thigh as I bring the leg back around. I think I've forgotten how to walk sometimes, as if my bones have turned brittle and could splinter apart like driftwood. My arms feel heavy, too, useless over-long ropes hanging slack at my sides. Cold air stings my throat and I swallow saliva endlessly to lubricate it, quickening my awkward pace until I am at last beyond the path and into the cove. I scramble over the rocks and land in a puff of sand.

They say it could drive a man mad, that endlessness. I run zigzag down to the edge, peeling off the espadrilles and flinging them up the slope. As I scrunch my toes into the sodden sand, I get grit under the nails and into the dry cracks on my heels.

I am not mad. I am just an onlooker as the sea gazes, infatuated, at the sky. The two are soulmates, embraced by the reclining shoreline and crowned by the cove. Butterflies erupt inside me as I stare out.

It won't be long until I really start showing. People will notice. Soon they may not let me swim. I think this is what bothers me most of all.

I am just about to pull the dress over my head when a rising chook-clunk, chook-clunk sound makes my head jerk. The trawlers are returning. I re-adjust myself, feeling annoyed. As the first boat sails past, I squint to pick out Bayard, who is gesticulating at the men on deck to organise the catch, obviously mindful of the approaching jetty. I have to breathe deeply as I watch him shoving shoulders aside to reach the writhing nets. Bayard has a strong stomach. I used to close my eyes whenever I saw the boats approaching, but imagining the haul – those undulating, slippery multitudes – gave way to visions worse than anything I could look at. So I watch, fixating on each of the three trawlers as they plug past the cove. I can breathe freely only when they have passed.

My stomach squeezes sickeningly for Bayard. I know that he'll be tearing back to market as soon as the haul is in, that I should be where he demanded, that I should tell him the truth. As if to agree, the little one flutters.

'I know, my love,' I murmur to my belly. 'But you're better off without him. We both are.'

Bayard and I stopped speaking after he joined the fishermen. He insisted it was necessary, that his age demanded work and that trawling demanded men. I swore that the hauls were cruel. It was nothing but slaughter, dredging the sea for every last edible creature, shredding delicate fins and tentacles in the vile netting. He sneered that I was insane. Screw loose. That he wished he'd never touched me.

I should tell him.

But the sea is an incurable temptress, inviting disobedience with its serpent-like hisses. Stripping bare, I slink into the shallows, then strike out, face down. I glug and splutter, breaking the surface, but below water I am already melting away, my taut limbs dissipating. I thrust my face under and the sea is instantly honey-sweet. I am a slip of silver and swim gleefully away.

Later, the market square is teeming. A corrosive stench begins at the docked trawlers and skulks between the stalls, where shining little corpses lie packed in ice.

'Luscious halibut, freshly caught! For you, darling, five eighty-five…'

'Squid's on special today, our lads hauled up a beauty… '

I tread slowly through the mass, trying to detach myself and let my eyeballs swim solo. It's no use: there are other eyes everywhere, glassy as marbles, catching mine; their scaly bodies gleam grey and bronze and gold, with ruby speckles where the nets have torn them.

'How about a treat for him indoors, love?'

A stall-holder proffers a hunk of flesh in my direction, leering hopefully. I veer away from the market and lurch towards the dock, where eager hands cast the last boxes along the jetty towards an iron shed.

As I approach, the shed door bangs open and a yellow-trousered backside emerges, bent over, dragging a bundle of nets. Its owner rights himself and shouts an unintelligible query into the shed. Bayard's indistinct instructions echo back from within, the sound of his voice churning my blood.

The fisherman nods and carries the netting away, whilst I cling to the corrugated iron, taking shallow, dry breaths. I want to bolt. I want to run right back to the cottage and slam the door. No, better, I want to swim. Right this minute. I could make it in three strides, over the wall, onto the jetty and under – but even if nobody saw me, the trawlers are still docked nearby, their nets blooming lazily below water.

I'd risk my life in a heartbeat, but not yours, little one.

Covering my belly, I step into the shed.

He's sitting on an upturned crate with his back to the door, elbows on his knees, making jerky arm movements. Every few moments something splats wetly at his feet, and he scoops the remains into a creel. I retch with horror.

Bayard whips round at the noise, sees me backing away and smirks. 'Lads, who let Nutso in?' he jeers, but the fishermen are outside, larking about as they sluice down the decks. Water trickles through the doorway and we both watch it awkwardly for a moment. Bayard's taunt hangs between us.

He had meant to surprise me with his new job, inviting me for a home-cooked meal to celebrate some 'good news'. He said he'd done something special for me, something that would alter our fortunes. The pie he placed in front of me had fish heads and tails sticking out of the pastry. Their slippery eyes gazed sadly at me. 'Caught them myself,' he'd boasted. 'I'll be making money from now on.' Misinterpreting my shocked silence, he explained it was Stargazy pie. 'It's tradition round here to keep the fish whole,' he beamed. 'So you can let their heads poke out to look at the stars.' Minutes later the pie was on the floor and he was calling me insane.

'Thought you weren't coming,' Bayard mutters now.

He's not grinning any more. I risk a glance upwards, and find defiance in his eyes. They're sparklingly blue, like the sea in summer, with translucent lashes that make him look rinsed out. His pale hair is newly short and stiff with salt. He used to wear it long, in a merman's ponytail that glistened to match my seaweed kinks. His face is belligerently bare and wind-scrubbed without it.

'Sorry to disappoint you.'

This is all wrong. He's wiping his hands on his undershirt and leaving red smudges. There are empty creels and nets stacked up around me, snakes of mooring line coiled against the back wall.

Tell me you don't want him, little one. Tell me, somehow.

'I need to say something,' I begin.

'Look, if this is about the trawling, save it. You've made yourself quite clear.'

'No, it's…'

'Because I've really had it,' he ploughs on, 'with the constant hassling and then the silence and now the hassling again. Maybe I don't like it either. Maybe I hate coming home stinking to high heaven, covered in fish guts –'

'I'm pregnant,' I say, and water roars in my ears.

It's filthy in here. The ground alone is greasy with blood and oil. Bayard's last, flaccid cadavers are heaped up in a crate, gaping, awaiting their disembowelment. I feel as if my own stomach has been knifed open and my guts slopped over the concrete.

'And?'

I can't look at him. He marches across to me and jerks my chin upwards so I have to make eye contact. The sharp reek of his fingers stings my nostrils. I can't turn my head.

'Mine?' he says curtly. I blink rapidly and try to nod. This seems satisfactory, as he lets go.

'Right.' He's pacing the shed now, kicking the mooring ropes back to the walls, shunting the nets into bundles that reopen instantaneously once left. I stand like an island and let him circle me, my arms clasped stiffly over my abdomen.

'So you hate the trawling,' he says, still striding about. 'You lose your mind over some stupid hauls –: people have got to eat, for goodness' sake. Then you ignore me for weeks because of it and now this happens.'

'I don't want anything.'

'What's happened to you?' He clutches exasperatedly at the air. 'I thought if I could just get some money together…'

'I don't want your money.'

He laughs scathingly. 'You want the money. Hell, you're going to need the money now. What else have you got?'

When I can't answer, his sardonic smirk reappears.

'This means you listen to me from now on,' he commands, leaning over the half-full crate before kicking it so that it skids across the concrete.

'If you want the baby…'

He dangles a fistful of dead fish in my face. I yelp and stagger backwards, gagging with the stench and the fluid dribbling out of its eye sockets.

'You get used to this!'

The fish eyes goggle balefully into mine. I launch out of the shed and choke up bile behind the door, then run blindly through the market and up the hill before Bayard can see my tears.

Later, Lucretia finds me in the hammock, one finger tracing my stomach. She's holding a steaming basin, another of her herbal therapies. I sit up and she sluices my feet in the murky soak, which smells gingery and prickles between my toes. The sky is darkening, and ribbons of moonlight glisten inside the basin. For as long as she's been lodging with me, I've let her practise whatever therapies she insists I need. I can tell she needs someone to look after.

'How is?' she asks, nodding towards my midriff.

I murmur non-committally.

'Boy,' she falters. 'Boy…bay?'

'Bayard?'

She blinks expectantly.

'We're on our own,' I say. She grunts, as if she expected it.

I glance at the cottage, where the blue stripe of the kitchen blind ripples against the unlocked window. Sea spray catches in my nostrils and my head lifts instinctively to taste the salt. Lucretia notices.

'No,' she barks, tugging my ankles and massaging roughly. 'No swim. Dark.'

I fidget. The ginger is making my blood fizz. What does it matter now?

I wait until she has risen and turned before I swing out of the hammock, force on my espadrilles and make a run for the slope. My muscles shriek in protest, joining Lucretia's remonstrative cries.

The sky is inky blue, but the shore is radiant under the moon and I can find my way easily. I can't wait to let go of my limbs, to release the tension in my joints. The water swoops up to meet me as I cast my clothes aside and plunge in. Night winds make the sea restless, so I let the current scoop me where it chooses, playfully twisting in a whirling dance. Chinks of silver moonlight skitter around the sea bed. I flit above gulping anemones and laces of seaweed, sea spiders spinning weightlessly into blackness. Leaning into the thrust sends tremors through my bones.

We can fly, little one, we are free.

A shadow swells above, moon-rimmed. It's night, so I'm especially wary, tensing up in order to avoid going closer.

It's a hull, right above me. The terror is electrifying and sends me shooting downwards, but a bulge of pressure flings me off course. Blood thrums in my head.

I shouldn't be here.

More shadows. There's a pendulum, a yellow light. I momentarily think of sunshine, but the water is still black.

The net swings into me and pain streaks across my spine.

I am so heavy. The sea sucks and gurgles. I writhe uselessly, tangling tighter with every thrash.

Someone's there. Two shapes sink down, coral pink, and swirl around searchingly.

A smack of cold. The yellow light reels across me, flinging the faces above into sharp relief. I know nothing but deep voices and fire in my gills.

The Writers

JOANNE HARRIS (MBE) was born in Barnsley in 1964, of a French mother and an English father. She studied Modern and Mediaeval Languages at Cambridge and was a teacher for fifteen years, during which time she published three novels, including *Chocolat* (1999), which was made into an Oscar-nominated film starring Juliette Binoche and Johnny Depp.

Since then, she has written fifteen more novels, two collections of short stories, a Dr Who novella, guest episodes for the game *Zombies, Run* and three cookbooks. Her books are now published in over fifty countries and have won a number of British and international awards. She is an honorary Fellow of St Catharine's College, Cambridge, has honorary doctorates in literature from the universities of Sheffield and Huddersfield, and has been a judge for the Whitbread Prize, the Orange Prize, the Desmond Elliott Prize and the Royal Society Winton Prize for Science.
www.joanne-harris.co.uk

TIM MAJOR's first novel, *You Don't Belong Here*, was published by Snowbooks in 2016. He has also released two novellas, *Blighters* (Abaddon, 2016) and *Carus & Mitch* (Omnium Gatherum, 2015) – the latter was shortlisted for a This Is Horror Award. His short stories have featured in *The Literary Hatchet*, *Interzone* and numerous anthologies, including *Best British SF 2017* and *Best Horror of the Year Volume 10*, edited by Ellen Datlow. Tim is co-editor of the British Fantasy Society's fiction journal, *BFS Horizons*.

Eqalussuaq was previously published in *Not One Of Us*.

CARMEN MARCUS lives and writes on the wild Yorkshire coast. As the daughter of a fisherman and Irish chef her writing brings together the practical and the magical. She is a poet and author. Her poetry has been commissioned by the BBC, Durham Book Festival and the Royal Festival Hall. Her debut novel *How Saints Die* was published in 2017 with Harvill Secker and tells the story of adult mental breakdown through the eyes of a child. The novel was longlisted for the Desmond Elliott Prize 2018

Bight, Tomcat and the Moon was previously published with Ashland Creek Press in 2016.

ALEX REECE ABBOTT. An Irish Novel Fair winner, and finalist in the Bath Novella-in-Flash Award, Alex is widely published and anthologised. Her stories have won the Arvon, Crediton and Northern Crime prizes and featured in the Word Factory's Citizen season. Among others, her work has shortlisted for the Bridport, Tillie Olsen, Lorian Hemingway, HG Wells, Maria Edgeworth, Fish, Aurora and Sunday Business Post Penguin short story prizes.
An earlier version of *The King Tide* was published in *Fortune: the HG Wells Short Story Anthology* (November 2014) and in Ireland, in the *Words on the Waves Anthology* in early 2015.
www.alexreeceabbott.info

LIZ WRIDE writes plays and short fiction. In 2014, her Dylan Thomas Centenary play *No 5 Cwmdonkin Drive* (produced by Welsh Fargo Stage Company) toured Wales and was performed at the Lost Theatre's One Act Festival. Her 2015 story, *Potato* was shortlisted for the 'Elle UK Talent Awards'. *Fillet* was shortlisted for Liar's League's 'Heads and Tails' competition in 2017.

PAULINE JÉRÉMIE was born and raised in France. She moved to Edinburgh to complete her master's in Creative Writing, and still lives and works in the Scottish capital. Her writing has been published in *From Arthur's Seat*, *The Ogilvie*, and *PENning Magazine*, and she recently performed her work at the 70th Edinburgh Fringe Festival.

SARAH LEAVESLEY is a poet, fiction writer, journalist, and editor at V. Press poetry and flash fiction imprint. Overton Poetry Prize winner 2015, she is author of four poetry collections, two pamphlets, a touring poetry-play and two novellas. Her poetry has been published by the *Financial Times*, the *Guardian, The Forward Book of Poetry 2016*, on Worcestershire buses and in the Blackpool Illuminations. She was longlisted for the New Welsh Writing Awards memoir prize in 2017 and the essay collection prize in 2018. Her flash fiction publications include pieces in *Jellyfish Review, Oxford Today, The Nottingham Review, Spelk, Flash: The International Short-Short Story Magazine* and *The Ofi Press Magazine*, including a Best Small Fictions nomination. Her novellas, *Kaleidoscope* and *Always Another Twist*, are also published by Mantle Lane Press.

SUSAN BARSBY lives in Nottingham with her husband and young daughter. By day she works for the city council and by night she writes novels, short stories and creative non-fiction. Her work has been published in *The A3 Review* and *DNA Magazine*, among others. She can be found on Twitter at @SusanEBarsby and occasionally blogging at Books from Basford https://basfordianwrites.com.

SARAH EVANS. Following a career first in theoretical physics and then economics, Sarah Evans unexpectedly found herself starting to write short stories. Over a hundred of these stories have won awards and/or been published in competition anthologies, journals and online, with publishing outlets including: the Bridport Prize, Unthank Books, Riptide, Shooter and Best New Writing. She has won a number of short story prizes, including Words and Women, Winston Fletcher, Stratford Literary Festival, Glass Woman and Rubery. She has also had work performed in London, Hong Kong and New York.

LINDA MACLENNAN originates from the Isle of Wight, a diamond-shaped island in southern England. She graduated with a First Class BA (Hons) in Writing Contemporary Fiction at Southampton Solent University, and a Distinction on the MA in Creative Writing at Southampton University. She has been successful in local, national and international writing competitions, winning second prize in the Amergin Creative Writing Awards, third prize in the Doris Gooderson Short Story Contest, long-listed three times in the Fish Short Story Competition, and appeared in the British Council's *Inspired by Tagore* anthology after entering their International Writing Competition. Having returned to the island three years ago she now lives in a former railway station.

LYDIA MCGILL has lived near the South coast all her life, which might be why she can't seem to stop writing stories about the sea. She works in the English office at a university, where she loves seeing students getting excited about literature. When not at work she can usually be found making terrible puns and trying to finish her novel.

Acknowledgements

This publication was supported using public funding by the National Lottery through Arts Council England.

Mantle Lane Press would like to acknowledge help and support from Writing West Midlands.

Mantle Lane Press is a subsidiary of Mantle Arts Limited, which receives financial support from North West Leicestershire District Council.